AVENGING ANGELENOS

BOOKS IN THIS SERIES

Sisters in Crime/Los Angeles Presents

AVENGING ANGELENOS

Edited by Sarah M. Chen, Wrona Gall,
and Pamela Samuels Young

Introduction by Frankie Y. Bailey

Down & Out Books
3959 Van Dyke Road, Suite 265
Lutz, FL 33558
DownAndOutBooks.com

Cover design by Alam Twaha

ISBN: 1-64396-204-3
ISBN-13: 978-1-64396-204-7

TABLE OF CONTENTS

PROLOGUE
Los Angeles, Spring 2021

Welcome to the Sisters in Crime/Los Angeles Chapter short story anthology, *Avenging Angelenos*. It has been my honor to serve as president of the chapter these past few years, and I am so proud of the people and the work that went into making this specific anthology happen.

The biennial anthology is one of my favorite benefits that we offer to our chapter members. Only chapter members can submit. For our new writers, it's an opportunity to get that all-important first credit. For many of our established writers, it's a chance to shake the stuffing out and try something different. For others, writing the short story is what they do and it's a chance to celebrate that.

Our stories are chosen blind, so that even the newest writer will not get lost. It's a complicated process and a lot of work for our committee to make sure that the stories get to our editors in a timely fashion. Our committee also must find those editors, which this year was no simple feat. Let's be real. The pandemic had so many of us freaking out that the thought of taking something on like this was just too much.

Pandemic or not, people need to meet, to connect, to find some measure of peace in the middle of chaos, and that's what a good short story can do. That's also what we try to do as Sisters in Crime. Our national organization is about inclusion and we do our best, in our own stumbling, faulty way, to comply. Our job is to offer support for our members and make sure that all voices are heard.

Which is another reason why this anthology is so important to me. It's another platform, another opportunity to let our members' voices be heard. Come hear what we have to say, then come join us and let us hear your story.

Anne Louise Bannon
President, Sisters in Crime/Los Angeles

Marie Stein
Henry Forman
Julia Bricklin
Sisters in Crime/Los Angeles
Anthology Committee

INTRODUCTION

Frankie Y. Bailey

Discussing the "psychological underpinnings" of revenge, a team of social scientists writes: "In Western societies, revenge is considered taboo; taking revenge is thought to be childish and unethical and the responsibility of the constitutional state only. Nevertheless, we seem to feel ambivalent about revenge. Those who do not avenge (and perhaps also forgive) are seen as weak or cowardly" (Grobbink et.al., 2015: 893).

This ambivalence about seeking retribution for a perceived wrong is also complicated by whether the retaliation is on behalf of oneself (seeking revenge) or someone else (avenging). In fact, this distinction is often ignored because avengers may feel they are acting not only for themselves but to rid the world of a "bad" person—or, at least, to neutralize that person's ability to do more harm.

Is an avenger also a vigilante? In the sense that we think of a vigilante as "taking the law into his or her own hands," then a person who carries out retribution rather than seeking the aid of law enforcement or other official state agencies would fall into this category, a subgenre of popular films (such as the *Death Wish* series) featuring "citizen vigilantes".

The motivation to seek personal revenge has several elements. Aside from actual physical harm, there is the sense of humiliation

3

(damage to self-esteem). Related to this is the belief that the harm is wrong and undeserved. Subsequently there is the drive to restore "equality of power." Together these elements provide the motivation to cause harm to the perceived perpetrator of this damage (Vol, 2003, cited in Grobbink. 2015).

Although it is human to feel anger toward someone who has done us harm, at what point does the desire for revenge become "pathological?" Is it when we begin to fantasize about acts of violence—or, when we take the first steps to act on those fantasies?

Whatever form it takes, retribution may be bittersweet—desired, achieved, but leaving the avenger feeling hollow or with a sense of loss. Instead of positive outcomes, such as recovered self-esteem and equilibrium, the avenger may suffer negative outcomes, such as additional trauma and involvement in the criminal justice system (Eadeh et al, 2017).

But—as the stories in this anthology demonstrate—when it comes to fiction both the writer and the reader can enjoy the delicious experience of a well-executed act of retribution. In the famous first line of Edgar Allan Poe's "The Cask of Amontillado" (*Godey's Lady's Book*, 1846), Montresor, the narrator, tells us: "The thousand injuries of Fortunato I had borne as I best could, but when he ventured upon insult I vowed revenge." He does not tell us the exact nature of the insult, but he has decided that Fortunato must be punished, and that he himself must get away with acting as his judge and jury. "I must not only punish but punish with impunity. A wrong is unredressed when retribution overtakes its redresser…"

It is the carnival season, and as we watch, the vengeful Montresor begins to put his plan into action. Pretending joviality, he leads the drunken Fortunato into the catacombs in search of a cask of amontillado. Before Fortunato realizes what is happening, he is imprisoned and being entombed in a crypt, among the bones of others who have died there.

The reader wonders how Fortunato could have insulted Montresor so gravely and yet be unaware of the harm he had done. How could he have believed that he and Montresor were friends? Is Montresor himself insane? A mad man who has exaggerated a minor offense and taken deadly retribution?

The narrator tells us in the final lines of the story that Fortunato has been buried there in the catacomb for decades. And he, the avenger, has gotten away with his crime.

Flowing from Poe's pen, this story is more horror than crime fiction.

But stories of retribution often have an element of horror, don't they?

Such stories are often laced with dark humor. For example, when the murder weapon is a frozen leg of mutton (Roald Dahl, "Lamb to the Slaughter" 1953) used to kill an offending husband, the leg is disposed of with the unwitting assistance of the investigating detectives themselves.

Dark humor and an avenger who believes there is no reason to "turn the other cheek" or to "forgive and forget"—these are the elements of the stories in this anthology. The other common denominator is the setting—these are "avenging Angelenos." In the City of Angels, these protagonists take wicked revenge on those who have done them wrong.

In "The Ink Well" by Kathy Norris, the dead man himself tells us that he was found floating face down in the surf back in 1952. To his frustration, he was attacked from behind. He does not know which of the several people who had reason to hate him exacted revenge. But in an epilogue, the reader learns that the avenger had a noble motive—and an old score to settle.

In "The Queen of Mean" by Paula Bernstein, the narrator faces a moral dilemma when a "mean girl" from her school days shows up in the hospital emergency room where the narrator is now a doctor. Does the fact that the mean girl—now a woman—shows no remorse for the bullying that led to a tragic death justify what the doctor is thinking of doing?

Peggy Rothschild's "The Magic Hour" is a twisty tale that will leave the reader saying, "Oh!" A mother who likes the hour of the day when children are tucked in their beds and sleeping quietly has more on her mind than having a few moments to herself.

Laurel Wetzork's "Gunning for Justice" is set during World War II and inspired by an actual event that occurred in Los Angeles in 1942. The protagonist finds herself in a situation that requires both grit and resourcefulness.

The avenger in Gay Toltl Kinman's "Best Served Cold" has waited ten years to make an arrogant publisher pay for the critique he didn't give her. As the publisher discovers, a writer with a grudge—and the time to work on her plot—can do serious damage.

Tarantulas play an important role in "Manny's Angel" by Jenny Carless. The protagonist wonders if she is being haunted. As the three other people involved in an old wrong die one-by-one, she wonders if she is next.

In Meredith Taylor's "Avenging Superheroes," the avengers are "Wonderous Woman" and her sidekicks. They come to the rescue of a family man who has gotten in over his head.

The red-haired, blue-eyed infant in Avril Adams's "The Baby" is an enigma. So is her mother, who is exhausted and anxious. As the mother's visiting friend tries to understand what is happening, she is drawn into an unusual alliance.

The British woman in "The Unkindest Cut" by L.H. Dillman writes a series of letters to her lover from prison. Over several months, she recounts her experience of incarceration and what brought her there as she hopes to regain her freedom.

"Funeral Games" by Hal Bodner focuses on the competition between rivals in the business of high-profile Hollywood funerals. The underhanded tactics of his rival prompt the protagonist to what he considers a fitting solution.

In "Christine Thirteen," Melinda Loomis's protagonist cele-brates her twenty-sixth birthday and decides it is time to find and punish the man who destroyed her life when she was a teenager. The final line of this story leaves the reader with a moral dilemma.

So, sit back and enjoy revenge served up with malice aforethought in this collection of short stories by imaginative and talented writers.

References

Eadeh, F., Peak, S.A., and Lambert, A.J. (2017) The bittersweet taste of revenge: On the negative and positive consequences of retaliation. *Journal of Experimental Social Psychology*, 68, 27-39.

Grobbink, L., Derksen, J., and van Marie, H. (2015) Revenge: An analysis of its psychological underpinnings. *International Journal of Offender Therapy and Comparative Criminology*, 59:8, 892-907.

THE INK WELL

Kathy Norris

On August 29, 1952, at seven twenty-two p.m., I was walking on Ink Well Beach, watching the sun sink below the horizon. I heard splashing behind me and thought it was my girl Portia. We were getting married on the beach the next day. But instead of Portia's warm arms, I felt a cold, sharp jab against the back of my neck, like a bee sting. Everything turned black except that red sun.

The next morning Portia found my dead body floating face down in the surf. I was still wearing the promise rings we'd exchanged back in high school.

My full name is Keondre Langston Woods, but I was better known as "Ken" or "The Kenster." In 1943 I was the first Negro to ever win the Triple Crown of Surfing, making me Surfer of the Year.[1] At the time I was only eighteen years old.

White Americans had a hard time pronouncing Keondre in 1943. Hell, they had a hard time with me, period: my skin color,

---

[1] The Triple Crown of Surfing actually started in 1983. http:\\vanstriplecrownofsurfing.com. Accessed 03-12-14. Nick Gabaldon (1927-1951) is widely considered the first documented surfer of African-American and Latino ancestry; however he is not credited with any surfing championships.
http: //en.wikipedia.org/wiki/Nick_Gabaldon. Accessed 03-12-14.

my attitude, my voice, which over the phone sounds white when I want it to.

They were willing to cut "Ken" a little slack; "Keondre," not so much.

The day I was murdered started out well enough. Portia didn't wake up when I crept in after partying late the night before. Portia and I have an understanding, but there's no sense rubbing the girl's face in it. Especially now that she's four months along. Those pregnancy hormones are a bitch. Besides, she knows she's The One. I was out of the house by five-oh-two, before she got up for her nursing gig, so we didn't get into it. I took her Chevy since my Mercury Woodie was low on gas.

As I rolled down Pacific Coast Highway, the radio announced the results of yesterday's game between the Brooklyn Dodgers and St. Louis Cardinals. I needed the Cardinals to win to cover the point spread, and they did. I pumped my first and yelled "Yes!" into the cool pre-dawn air. I had big money riding on the Cardinals. I owed money all over town and was tired of running into people whose faces turned hard when they saw me.

I ran into my old surfing coach, Bill Spivey, in the parking lot on the Palos Verdes bluffs overlooking the Pacific Ocean. I hadn't seen Bill in years, but his craggy features stood out against the flock of youthful faces. As usual, I was the only raisin in the sugar bowl.

"Spivey!" I cried, clapping him on the back. "I thought you were in Australia, man! What brings you back to the wild, wild west?"

Bill jumped at my touch. "Kenster?" he said. "I didn't see the Woodie in the parking lot, or I'd have looked for you. What happened to my car?" Spivey had lost his Woodie to me in a poker game before heading to Australia. "And what brings you this far south?" he said. I continued to smile, but felt the hair rise on the back of my neck. What was it I heard in his voice?

Reading between the lines of friend and foe was second nature to me. Was Bill implying I shouldn't surf the whites-only beaches of Palos Verdes? Or simply making an observation? My shoulders slumped; this guessing game was exhausting. The only time I was free of it was riding the waves. Mother Nature's ass-kickings were colorblind.

"Yeah," I said, "but the PV forecast is for five-to-seven-foot swells, much better than in my neck of the woods. Thought I'd check it out."

We were silent for a moment. Bill turned away first, looking out over the ocean. A light offshore wind had kicked in with the dawn, and the swells were moving west northwest.

"What do you think?" he said. "Seventeen seconds?" He was asking me to estimate the swell period, or time between waves. I was not so easily distracted.

"Maybe" I said. "What brings you to L.A., man?" I repeated. "Between the waves and those Australian babes, I thought I'd seen the last of your ass."

The Bill Spivey I knew loved talking about women, but this man remained silent. Suddenly he was in motion, gathering up his gear.

"Gotta run," he said, slinging his bag over his shoulder.

"What?" I said, grabbing his arm. "You just got here!"

He tried to shake me off. "Look, Kenster" he said, "I really gotta move. Catch you later."

"When?" I demanded, not letting go of his arm. I don't know what got into me; the mellow Kenster never pressed. But something was off. Bill Spivey had been my mentor and best friend; now he wouldn't give me the time of day.

Bill looked down at my brown hand gripping his white arm. Through my fingers you could see his grinning dolphin tattoo.

"Noon today," he said finally, licking his lips. "Lifeguard Tower 28."

I let the dolphin go.

Paddling out to meet the waves, I thought about where and when I'd fallen in love with surfing. It was 1948, and the Ink Well was the most popular colored beach in Southern California.

Segregated beaches ended in 1927, so in theory a colored man could go to any beach in Southern California: Redondo, Palos Verdes, Playa Vista, take your pick. But in reality, any Negro who laid his blanket on sand that wasn't between Bay and Bicknell Streets in Santa Monica was asking for trouble. That stretch of sand was called the Ink Well.[2]

When I was seven years old, I taught myself to surf at the Ink Well. It's the perfect beginners' beach, with gentle, foamy waves coming in parallel to shore. Using a discarded longboard, I practiced on the sand, mimicking the white surfers I'd seen at Venice Beach.

Eventually I learned to ride the waves lying flat on my board, not standing up. Bill taught me how to "pop-up" and assume the classic surfing stance. I thought about Bill as I headed to the Pancake Palace after my morning surf. Surfing usually cleared my mind, but not today. My timing had been off, and I'd bottomed out more often than not. I had the bruises on my right shoulder to prove it.

My brother Walter was waiting when I arrived. Steady Walter had the same breakfast every day; oatmeal and orange juice, followed by a handful of vitamins. You'd think he'd be in good shape, as picky as he is about food. But at thirty-two Walter had a spare tire and man boobs.

"Heh, Chubs," I said, sliding into our usual booth.

"Don't call me that," he said, but there was no heat behind it. He looked up from the papers scattered around the table. His big brown eyes were his best feature, but behind his thick glasses they looked round and slightly fishy. He had on his uniform, a conservative dark suit, white shirt, and plain tie. What can I say? My older brother was a born accountant.

Rachel, our usual waitress, placed a mug of coffee and toast

---

[2] The Ink Well.
http: //en.wikipedia.org/wiki/Santa_Monica_State_Beach. Accessed 03-12-14.

with jam in front of me. I ordered hotcakes, double bacon and eggs, and orange juice. Walter licked his lips as he listened to my order.

"Don't look at me," I said to him. "It's not my fault I can eat anything I want and stay pretty." I thumped my chest. "Pure muscle," I said. I reached over and patted Walter's. "Pure fat. You need to hit the gym, bro."

"I'll hit the gym when you become a C-P-A," he said. "You'd be broke without me handling your business, and don't you forget it."

Here we go again, I thought. Walter was family. Walter also needed a job. He'd been hanging around me like a puppy dog anyway, so I'd let him play at being my manager. He'd taken my winnings and turned them into what he called an "income stream." It wasn't much, but it saved the two of us from a nine-to-five slave. All I had to do was keep winning. But the competition was getting younger every year.

As if he'd read my mind, Walter said, "I heard from the West Coast Surfing Championship yesterday."[3]

Oh shit, I thought.

"They tell me you've pulled out of the trials."

I chewed my toast and took a sip of coffee. "Yeah, I'm taking some time off."

"It didn't occur to you to let your manager know?"

"I'm getting married tomorrow. Portia wants a honeymoon and all that. I promised her I'd take some time off."

"Are you crazy? I worked my ass off to get you into the trials in the first place!" Walter was building to a full head of steam. "You haven't exactly been burning up the waves lately."

"I'm still healing from the wipeout at the Pipeline Masters in

---

[3] The West Coast Surfing Championship began in 1959. In 1964 it became the US Open of Surfing.
http: //en.wikipedia.org/wiki/U.S._Open_of_Surfing. Accessed 03-12-14.

Hawaii," I said tightly.[4] I relived the nightmare. The enormous fifty-foot surf. My head thudding against something hard on the ocean floor. Blacking out.

"Your last big win was two years ago," Walter said, his words interrupting my memories. "We need this one."

I looked at him. "We? I don't see your ass out there on the pipeline, bro."

"We're a team," Walter said. He actually believed it.

"No, we are not a team," I said. Really, I had let this manager bullshit go on too long. "I'm the one training 24/7, I'm the one risking my neck on killer waves, and I'm the one winning the money. My money. Give me a fucking break." Even I heard the strain in my voice.

Walter heard it, too. He put his hands up and softened his tone. "I know, Keondre, I know. You're tired, big man. But I have a plan. A way to get us out from under."

"What are you talking about?" I said.

Walter pushed his plate aside and folded his hands on the table.

"Ever hear of Esther Williams?" he said.

"MGM's Million Dollar Mermaid? The one who stars in all those water musical movies?" I said. "Who hasn't heard of Esther Williams?"

"She wasn't always a movie star," Walter said. "She got into movies after winning swimming championships."

"What's that got to do with me?" I asked.

Walter looked at me and sighed. "If Esther Williams can go from athlete to movie star, so can you."

I stared at Walter. "Do I look like a beautiful young white woman to you?"

He laughed. "No, you most certainly do not." He grew quiet. "But the time is right. Dodger revenues have skyrocketed since

---

[4] The Pipeline Masters is one of the three competitions that make up the Triple Crown of Surfing. See end note i.

14

they signed Jackie Robinson, and other franchises are taking notice." Jackie Robinson had broken the Major League Baseball color barrier five years ago when he signed with the Brooklyn Dodgers. My man. I made a point of betting on the Dodgers whenever I could.

Walter leaned in closer. "What I'm about to tell you is hush-hush. Can you keep your mouth shut?"

I rolled my eyes, but nodded yes. Walter's voice grew even softer, forcing me to lean in. "I didn't tell you because nothing's set, but I've been talking to Paramount about you. They're interested." He leaned back, grinning.

My heart sank. Another one of Walter's crazy schemes. I'd dodged the last one, something to do with selling advertising space on my swimming trunks. My swimming trunks, can you believe it! I'd look all kinds of crazy running around with someone else's name stitched to my behind. Labels go inside your clothes. Everybody knows that.

"Interested in what, exactly," I asked.

"Interested in a surfing movie, with you as the lead. You've got the right look, you're articulate when you want to be, and you're a winner. Or used to be. A West Coast Surfing Championship win would clinch the deal."

I stared at him. "You're telling me that all I have to do is win one more surfing competition, and I get the lead in a Paramount movie?"

Walter cleared his throat. "It's not that simple. They're looking at others, but you're the only Negro in the mix."

"What others?"

"The usual suspects. Bud Chapman, but he puts the 'ugh' in ugly. Johnson's been mentioned, but he doesn't have your track record. And Spivey."

"Spivey?" I repeated. Walter mistook my surprise for concern. "Nothing to worry about," he said, "Spivey's a little long in the tooth, you ask me."

He leaned forward. "You can go on a honeymoon anytime,

Keondre. Portia's put up with your bullshit for how long? She's not going anywhere."

I shook my head. "Sorry, man, but this sounds like another one of your crackpot ideas. They always blow up, and I'm always the one left holding the bag." Walter started to protest, but I cut him off.

"I've been meaning to talk to you anyway. I'm getting married tomorrow."

"I know that," Walter said. "And Portia's expecting. That's why I had you sign that life insurance policy the other day. If you have another surfing accident, they'll be set for life."

I didn't remember signing a life insurance policy. But Walter had shoved a lot of papers in my face at breakfast, and I'd tried to sign them before my eggs got cold.

"Walter, after you take your cut, I barely have enough to make ends meet," I said. "I have a family to take care of now. The way I see it, Portia can handle the business end. Sorry bro, but after the wedding, I have to cut you loose."

Rachel chose that moment to bring my order. She usually stops and chats, but one look at Walter's face and she fled. Steam rose from the hotcakes, and butter and syrup dripped down the sides. I stared at my food, mesmerized.

"You can't be serious," Walter said. His voice was barely a whisper.

I grabbed my knife and fork and dug into the hotcakes. Delicious. I know this sounds hard and all, stuffing my face with pancakes after firing my brother. But being a selfish bastard is part of my charm.

"Sorry, bro. Nothing personal," I continued. "We had a good run, but like the Bible says, all good things must come to an end." I swallowed a few more pancakes and helped myself to some bacon.

"The Bible doesn't say that," Walter said, staring at me.

"Whatever," I said, waving my hand dismissively in the air. "See, that's your problem, Walter. You lose focus. Stop worrying about who said what and focus on getting a new job. This gig is up." I looked at my watch. "Gotta run," I said, "thanks for breakfast." I was out the door before he could say another word.

I had money coming from my Dodgers win, so I headed over to Crescent Bay Park, a small strip of green bordering the Ink Well to the east.

Back in the day, the Ink Well had something for everyone. Families stretched their blankets on the warm sand, forming miniature fiefdoms bordered by colorful throws and pillows. Young couples strolled the boardwalk in matching white trousers and shirts, thin black belts wrapped around thinner waists. I grinned. Those pretty young things wouldn't dream of getting their freshly pressed hair wet. Seniors claimed the benches under the palm trees in Crescent Bay Park. They dozed, gentle breezes ruffling the pages of the Watts Times on their laps.

Eugene, my bookie, didn't have an office. He transacted business at the park, using whatever car he had at the time. Eugene changed cars the way other men changed clothes.

I found him parked in the narrow alley between the park's restrooms and the Casa del Mar Motel, leaning against an emerald green Cadillac DeVille hardtop. I should've known something was up when I saw his bodyguard Pookie with him. How he got the nickname Pookie nobody knows, but at six-foot-five and three-hundred pounds, no one asks.

Eugene, on the other hand, was a fragile grasshopper of a man who looked thinner and more brittle each time I saw him. One day he'd just dry up and blow away.

I'd started placing bets with Eugene three months ago, after I had trouble with Hastings. Hastings never could get a bet right. His bad memory cost me hundreds. Not that it mattered; Hastings or Eugene, they both worked for Mr. King, as mean and ruthless a son of a bitch as they come.

"Eugene!" I cried. I made a show of sniffing the air. "I smell cash money. Whatcha got for me, bro?"

Eugene's smile was sour. "You're kidding, right? As much as

you owe? Yesterday's win barely covers the vig. And a good thing, too. One more missed payment, and your surfing days are over."

"What vig?" I said. This couldn't be happening.

"The interest, the scratch, the extra cheese, you know what I'm talking about," Eugene said. "What, you thought the meter wasn't running on all those missed payments? Think again, my friend". He paused the way people do when they're about to say something profound.

"Interest Never Sleeps," he said reverently, punctuating each word with his hands. "It's a beautiful thing." Eugene sighed and gazed wistfully into space, as if interest was a lovely angel smiling down on him from heaven.

"Now," he said looking back at me, all business, "We take payment in anything beginning with a 'B.' Bills," he said, and then nodded at Pookie. "Or Broken Bones. Take your pick."

"Try bullshit!" I said, clenching my fists. I'd gone from happy to hot in a heartbeat, my stomach turning as sour as Eugene's smile. It was all too much—my injury, the nightmares, the debts, the baby, the wedding. And now this fool telling me he wouldn't hand over the cash I needed to pay for Portia's wedding ring. No way.

I didn't think, just put all my weight behind a brutal uppercut to Eugene's smirking face. I had the satisfaction of hearing bones crunch beneath my fist before Pookie was on me.

The fact that I'd gotten to his employer before he could stop me didn't help matters. Now Pookie had to make an example of me. He started with a left hook to my kidneys. I doubled over in blinding pain. So long spleen, I thought as he kicked me to the ground, sat on me, and hammered punches into my body with metronomic regularity. He seemed almost bored. I could hear Eugene cursing and swearing in the background.

I was about to pass out when I heard the unmistakable sound of a shotgun being racked. Pookie heard it, too. His fist stopped mid-air.

"That's right," said a quivery male voice. "Get off that young man and put your hands in the air."

Pookie did as he was told. My burning lungs sucked in air as his enormous bulk lifted off my ribs. Hallelujah.

"You too," the voice said to Eugene.

"This ain't no western, grandpa," Eugene said. "You better put that gun down before somebody gets hurt."

"I ain't your grandpa, boy. If I was, you'd know better than to peddle wickedness in my park. Don't know what's worse, the drugs or the gambling." He shook his head and spat in the dirt. "Don't tell me Satan ain't alive and kickin'. Now, put your hands against the wall. Don't make me ask again." The old man aimed the shotgun at Pookie and Eugene. Both men turned and placed their hands on the motel wall.

The quivery voice said to me, "Can you walk, son?"

I raised my head and got a good look at the old geezer. He was one of those vigilantes that patrolled the park, armed and dangerous...if only in his own mind. The gun probably wasn't even loaded.

But I'm not one to look a gift horse in the mouth. My left eye was swollen shut, and I could barely stand. "I can't see," I said.

"I didn't ask if you could see, I asked if you could walk," the old man said. "Hold on to my arm." He led me away, the shotgun trained on Eugene and Pookie. He was a frail old thing, but that shotgun never wavered.

"Wait a minute," I said, and limped back to Eugene.

"This ain't no time to socialize, son," the old man warned.

"Just keep the gun aimed at their nutsacks," I said, loud enough for both men to hear. I came up behind Eugene and eased my hand into his back pocket, pulling out a thick billfold. His back went rigid with rage.

"You're a dead man," he hissed between clenched teeth.

"Tell me something I don't already know," I said, removing the cash and dropping his wallet to the ground.

* * *

In exchange for a generous donation to the Temple of Deliverance Victory Faith C.O.G.I.C.,[5] the old man agreed to drive me to Watts. The thought of Eugene's blood money sponsoring churchly good works cracked me up.

He dropped me off at Portia's mother's house on East 103rd and Avalon in Watts. Grace Markham was hosting the rehearsal dinner, or rehearsal lunch in this case. The tiny two-bedroom house was packed with family, friends, and people I'd never seen before.

I tried sneaking around the back to clean up, but my nephew Antoine spotted me as the old man drove away. "There he is!" he yelled. "Uncle Keondre!" He and a pack of little crumb-snatchers surrounded me. Antoine wrapped his chubby seven-year-old arms around my legs. I tried to pick him up, but the stitch in my side kicked in. I hobbled to the front door like the pied piper, children in tow.

Sound poured from every door and window of the small house. Buffet tables crowded the front porch, and I could smell fried chicken and potato salad coming from the kitchen. The radio competed with the new television, the first on the block. Both were drowned out by the sound of a roomful of people talking all at once.

But after I limped in, you could have heard a pin drop. As if on cue, everyone turned to look at me, taking in my bloody swimming trunks, my black eye, and the assorted bruises covering my body. Portia's Aunt Shirley stared at me open-mouthed. Uncle Bill's mouth formed one grim line; uppity bastard never did like me. Floyd and Minnie White, friends of the family or cousins (I never could keep Portia's family straight), looked at each other and pulled their sons Anthony and Jay closer. Aunt Vilean, the family gossip, watched with glittering eyes, highball

---

[5] COGIC-Church of God in Christ

20

in hand. Grandma Higgins applied her cane to any backside that blocked her view. The assembled guests could not have looked more horrified if I'd pulled down my drawers and taken a dump in the middle of the living room.

Portia and her mother made their way through the crowd, Grace wiping her hands on her apron. "Here he is!" cried Portia, slipping her arm through mine. She's a big woman, and in heels looks me dead in the eye. She wore a festive red halter dress that revealed her gorgeous shoulders. She flashed me a look from those enormous brown eyes, and I knew she was pissed. But Portia kissed me on the cheek and announced to the crowd, "Keondre always did know how to make an entrance."

The tension in the room lightened as everyone laughed. Everyone except one woman I didn't recognize, a babe with the kind of figure that catches a man's eye—even if he has only one working at the time. Her gaze was so hard it could turn a man to stone.

Portia continued, "Everyone, please meet the love of my life, and father-to-be of our baby, Keondre Langston Woods."

That's my Portia! Once she mentioned the baby, everybody forgot about me. Walter, the only one from my side of the family at the party, hustled me upstairs.

"What the hell happened to you?" he asked, closing the bedroom door.

"What does it look like?" I snapped. "Got anything on you?" Walter pulled out his hip flask and handed it over.

"It looks like you got mugged," he said. I poured a shot of Jack down my throat. Just what the doctor ordered.

"Look again," I said, tossing Eugene's money on the bed. Walter counted the cash and whistled. I took another swig.

"Where'd this come from?" he asked. I started to lie, but what the hell.

"I took if off Eugene when he tried to punk me." I drained the rest of the flask and headed for the bathroom.

"Eugene, the bookie?" Walter squeaked. "One of Mr. King's boys?"

"The one and only," I said, spreading shaving cream over those parts of my face that weren't a pulpy mess. Walter covered his face with both hands. I tuned out his whining while I finished shaving. Finally, he left to pick up Portia's ring.

After a hot bath and a change of clothes, I felt almost human. The Jack didn't hurt either. I opened the door and ran into the beautiful babe with the stony gaze I'd spotted earlier. There was something familiar about her.

"Do I know you?" I asked. It was dark in the hallway, but I saw her roll her eyes. Playing hard to get. I like that in a woman. I leaned in close and put my arm against the wall, boxing her in. I looked deep into her eyes; women can't resist my soulful eyes.

"You don't remember me, do you?" she said.

"A man doesn't forget a woman like you," I said, but suddenly I wasn't so sure.

"Aren't you getting married tomorrow?" she whispered.

"Portia and I, we have an understanding," I said. "We're secure enough in our love to give each other space." I reached out and touched one of the spit curls framing her face.

"What about the other women? Do they understand?" Her eyes shifted suddenly, as if something had crept up behind me. I whirled around. Nothing. I looked back at her, frowning.

"What? You don't see them?" the mystery woman said, slipping deftly beneath my arm and out of reach. "That line of 'other women' behind you, with knives in their hands and revenge in their hearts?" Her soft, warm laugh was intoxicating.

"What's your number?" I said. "I'll call you when I get back."

"From your honeymoon? You are a bad boy."

"At least give me a name," I said as she headed down the hall.

She paused. "Call me Cookie," she said over her shoulder.

"See you later, Cookie."

"No, you won't," she said, and switched down the hall.

Portia was tired, so we made our excuses and left. Walter drove as I sipped on the Hennessy I'd snuck from the kitchen.

The car was stuffed with Portia's wedding gown, my tux, and all the stuff you need to say "I do" these days. You ask me, colored folks should go back to jumping the broom.

Portia dropped the "happy couple" act the moment we pulled away from the curb. She didn't look at me, and my conversational gambits were met with a snippy "yes" or "no." I sighed and looked out the window. I missed the old Portia.

Old Portia would've yelled and screamed and gotten it out of her system. And the make-up sex? Unbelievable. Pregnant Portia, on the other hand, was a smoldering volcano that might erupt at any moment. If this was married life, you could have it.

By the time Walter dropped us off it was five in the evening. Only then did I remember my meeting with Spivey. He probably didn't show. Flaky was Spivey's middle name.

In the meantime, Mount Portia had grown even more volatile. I had to act fast. My girl loves bonfires on the beach, so I told her I'd build one at the Ink Well and we'd watch the sunset together. Portia smiled and covered my face with little kisses. She went to get the blankets, and I headed for the beach.

You know the rest.

You probably think I'm angry about dying, a young man snuffed out in the prime of life and all. Murdered the day before his wedding to his high school sweetheart. Baby on the way. Bright Hollywood future. That's how it read in the *Los Angeles Times*. Like a tragedy.

But surfing teaches you that life is as ephemeral as the wave beneath your board. Truth be told, my act would've caught up with me sooner or later. If it hadn't been the surfing, it would've been the gambling, and if it hadn't been the gambling, it would've been the women. Or the booze. Portia would've gotten tired of my act and left with the kids. And without Walter looking after my finances, I'd probably end up broke.

Instead, I went out at the top of my game.

I have only one question, one bit of unfinished business. Which one of the losers in my life had the stones to take me out?

My brother Walter? Walter had the killer instinct of a June bug. Eugene and Pookie would have taken me out in a heartbeat, but they hadn't known I'd be at the beach that night. Could it be Spivey, trying to thin out the competition? But Spivey wouldn't take the fight to you, preferring to stab you in the back and slither away. Who then? I'd never know, and that pissed me off.

EPILOGUE

Lieutenant Angela Markham extended her leave from the Women's Army Corp to attend Keondre Woods's funeral. His death made the reunion with her dear friend Portia, whom she hadn't seen in seven years, bittersweet. And although she wanted to stay longer to support Portia, she couldn't. The Korean War was in its second year, and her nursing skills were in high demand.

"Do you have to go?" Portia asked as she drove her old friend to the airport.

"We can't sit by and let the Communists take over the world," Angela said. "The strong must protect the weak."

Tears welled in Portia's eyes. "I don't know how I'm going to get by without Keondre," she said. "And now you're leaving, too."

"The only thing necessary for the triumph of evil, is for good men to do nothing," Angela said softly.

"Who are you quoting this time?" Portia said.

"Edmund Burke, Irish statesman and philosopher, around the 1700s," Angela said.

The two women hugged farewell. As Lieutenant Markham boarded the Army C-46 Commando cargo plane, a medic from her M.A.S.H. unit greeted her.

"Heh, Cookie!" he said, "I thought you flew back last week!"

"Change of plans. I had to go to a funeral," Angela "Cookie"

Markham said. The medic nodded his head sympathetically. "Man plans, God laughs," he agreed.

Cookie buckled her seatbelt and the powerful plane roared down the runway. As it banked over the Pacific, it occurred to her she was looking down at the same waves the debauched deadbeat Keondre Woods had mastered so artfully.

She smiled. The syringe of cyanide had done its job. And while the loss of her nursing kit would mean endless paperwork, it was a small price to pay. To protect the weak.

THE QUEEN OF MEAN

Paula Bernstein

I put on my blue paper bonnet, my shoe covers, my N95 mask, and pulled a pair of latex gloves over the wrists of my surgical gown. I was lucky to have my own small supply of masks, which I'd purchased during the Getty fire, when the whole Westside was engulfed in smoke. Most of my fellow physicians, assigned to help in the Emergency Room, had to make do with regular surgical masks, and we were rapidly running low. I'd never encountered anything as terrifying as the Covid-19 epidemic. Los Angeles had turned into a ghost town.

The last item of my outfit was a plastic face shield. The ER had just gotten a supply. I hated it. It was hard enough to breathe through an N95 mask. Dealing with the fog that my breath created on the inside of the shield was yet another annoyance. I had nightmares about the virus sneaking under the shield and finding a defect in my mask. I took it off, wiped it clear with a surgical towel, and glared at it.

My left brain reminded me that the face shield would help protect me from getting infected and might even save my life. Healthcare workers were dropping right and left. There was no way I could do my job while maintaining social distance from patients. I had to get close enough to listen to their lungs. I took a few deep breaths, pretended it was a fashion statement, and replaced the shield on my head. It was time to stop being frightened and report to the ER.

The hospital emergency room was almost unrecognizable. There was a screening station in the parking lot, triaging patients with fevers or suspicious symptoms to one tent; patients with trauma, heart attacks or strokes to the inner sanctum; and severely ill patients, who were immediately tested for Covid-19, to that section of the ER that had been literally converted into a respiratory care unit. The assumption was that everyone could be carrying Covid, even those patients who supposedly were here for other emergencies.

The waiting room, normally packed solid, was almost empty, with seats spaced six feet apart. People with no health insurance and no primary care doctors—who often used the ER for colds, flu, diarrhea and other ailments—were scared, and staying away. Everyone else was either too sick to wait, or not sick enough to be admitted.

The exam spaces in the respiratory section had been remodeled as negative-pressure rooms, to prevent virus-laden air from infecting the rest of the ER. Doors and barriers had been constructed, isolating each pod of rooms like an airlock. I was the ER doctor assigned to the patients in rooms one through four.

Every time I entered an exam room to evaluate a new patient, my stomach clenched with fear. Would this be the carrier who would give me the virus and endanger my life? Anyone, the old man with chest pain, the teenager with appendicitis, or, in this case, the woman who'd been in a fender bender with an Amazon delivery truck, could be the one. I'd been literally living in the hospital for weeks, sleeping in an on-call room, so as not to risk infecting my husband. I took another deep breath, pushed against the door with my elbow, and went in to see the woman in room number three.

She was lying on a gurney, a neck brace supporting her head, dried blood on her face from a cheek laceration. A nasal cannula delivered supplemental oxygen. As I stepped closer, I recognized her, a thirty-year-old version of the girl I remembered from high school. Her blonde hair was artfully highlighted, her lips plumped, her striking blue eyes adorned with false eyelashes. A diamond the size of Montana glittered on her left ring finger.

I was glad I was wearing a mask, although even without one, Jennifer Gilbert wouldn't have recognized me. I'd always been invisible to Jennifer and her high school clique of the prettiest girls. I was almost tempted to rip off my mask so she could see the contempt and hatred on my face.

"I'm Dr. Silvers. How are you feeling?"

She wouldn't know the name. It was my husband's. Yes, I'm a feminist, but if your maiden name was Wiskowski, you would change it, too.

Jennifer didn't reply.

"Let me take a quick look at your vital signs."

I sat down at the computer terminal at the far end of the room, cleaned the keyboard with a disinfectant wipe, and pulled up her chart. Like all trauma patients, she'd had a total body CT scan for broken bones and internal bleeding. No sign of either, but I saw something far worse.

Jennifer's temperature had spiked to one-hundred-three degrees, her heart rate measured one-hundred-five, and she was breathing at a rapid thirty breaths per minute, despite the high flow of oxygen. Her lungs looked like ground glass. There was no doubt in my mind about the diagnosis, even without the results of her Covid-19 test. The pulse oximeter read a peripheral oxygen of ninety-one percent This was significantly below normal. I doubted she could sustain the rapid breathing rate required to deliver even this inadequate oxygen supply.

"I was driving myself to the hospital..." Her raspy voice paused for breath. "Had an accident." She punctuated her sentence with a chest rattling cough. "I have it, don't I?"

I could see misery in every line of her face as she tried to draw in oxygen through the plastic tubes in her nose. I helped her to roll over onto her left side so that I could listen to her lungs. Barely any breathing sounds registered in the lower lobes.

"Your test results aren't back yet, but you do have pneumonia. We'll admit you as soon as a bed is available. I'll have a respiratory therapist come in to help you with your breathing."

The therapist would probably switch her to a non-rebreathing mask or CPAP, but she would need a ventilator pretty soon. The ER was packed solid with Covid patients and the ICU was fully occupied. She wouldn't get a ventilator unless someone died.

"I'm starting you on a combination of anti-viral drugs that should be helpful," I said.

A recent clinical trial, published in the British medical journal *Lancet*, suggested that patients recovered faster with a triple antiviral combination. The ER staff had just begun using it because Remdesivir, the only FDA drug approved for the purpose so far, was in short supply, and as usual, the administration had failed to be either competent or transparent in its distribution to hospitals. My theory was the drug was only going to Red states. In any case, I wrote orders to start her on the combination cocktail.

I saw no need to examine her further and put myself at even greater risk. It wouldn't change her treatment. Her cheek could use a few stitches, but it wasn't actively bleeding at the moment, and if she wound up with a nasty scar, I wouldn't shed any tears. I excused myself and went on to the adjacent exam room to treat the next patient.

Twelve Years Earlier

Every high school has its mean girls. Beverly Hills High was no exception. My class had the Js—Jennifer, Jessica and Janice.

Jennifer was the queen bee, and the others orbited and followed her lead in all things.

Jennifer established her dominance freshman year. She was a statuesque blonde in designer jeans and skin-tight T-shirts with a mouth that spouted venom, verbally and on social media. I learned to avoid her like the plague.

Most of her venom was directed at the second tier of girls who aspired to be part of her clique, or who dared to compete for the attention of the hottest guys on campus. I was not one of them.

I hid in the back of class, wearing oversized tunics that obscured my midriff bulge, kept my mouth mostly shut, did my homework, and got As on all my exams. I needed great grades to get into college, and after college into medical school. I'd known that I was going to be a doctor from the time I was ten years old.

I lived in the slums of Beverly Hills, south of Olympic, in a modest duplex that my grandparents had bequeathed to my mother. My dad owned a local pharmacy. Mom stayed home and nurtured their three children. I was the oldest and the most ambitious.

Visiting my father in the afternoons was the genesis of my interest in medicine. I'd sit at the pharmacy counter, drinking a cherry coke, or sometimes a black and white ice cream soda, and watch as he dispensed medication to his customers.

"What's that for? What kind of disease is that? How does the medicine fix it?" I found everything he did fascinating.

"Are you going to be a pharmacist when you grow up?" he would tease, his kind smile enhancing his double chin.

"I think I'll be a doctor and write the prescriptions," I said. "That way I can figure out what's wrong with people and make them better."

If no one was waiting at the counter, he'd lean over and deposit a kiss on my forehead.

"I think you'll make a great doctor."

His endorsement was a relief because I couldn't imagine myself at home like my mother, trying to corral two rambunctious young boys and constantly cooking. My life had to be more interesting than that.

I made a few casual friends in high school, mostly misfits like myself who were not competitive in the popularity contest. My friends were all too nerdy, too fat or too ethnic to be worthy of consideration. Occasionally, we sat together in the cafeteria but more often I ate alone, absorbed in a book. I didn't mind. I found books more interesting than people, and I'd always been able to keep myself entertained. When I saw couples walking hand-in-hand through the halls, I regretted not having a boyfriend, but I doubted that I'd ever be pretty enough to attract one. No one would ever propose marriage to me, so I made plans to support myself. I was not going to depend on anyone else. Ever.

During my senior year, a new girl named Peggy transferred into our class from a school on the East Coast. Peggy was clearly going to be even lower than I was on the popularity scale. I was merely overweight. Peggy was obese, with a thick New York accent. I wondered how long it would take for the Js to obliterate her.

I was sitting alone in the cafeteria the second week of school when someone asked, "Is it okay if I sit here?"

Peggy, carrying a lunch tray, smiled at me. She had a dazzling smile, and a pretty, round face with large brown eyes, fair skin, and perfect teeth. Her face was plump with a significant double chin, but that day I didn't notice. The warmth of her smile mesmerized me.

"Sure, I'm Meredith. You're the new girl, right?" I could only imagine how hard it must be to switch schools in your senior year. "Rumor has it that you're from New York."

"Scarsdale," she said. "My dad's law firm transferred him to the L-A office, so we had to move."

"That must've been hard," I said. "I'm sure you miss your friends."

"A lot." Peggy opened up a container of yogurt and began eating it. "It isn't easy to make new ones. I imagine everyone here has enough friends. I'll probably have to wait until college when we're all in the same boat."

My heart went out to her. "There's always room for another friend."

"To tell the truth, I didn't have many friends in Scarsdale. Most of the kids were part of a clique and wouldn't hang out with anyone who wasn't in their group."

"It's like that here, too. Most of the girls have too much money and too many clothes."

Peggy turned to glance at some of the long tables where groups of attractive girls and handsome boys were seated together, talking and laughing. Some were clearly couples, the boys possessively draping their arms around their girlfriends. There was an Asian table, and smaller African-American and Latino tables. The Iranian students were a particularly large group and had their own sub-cliques. These students ate together and stayed in their ethnic lanes. Most were nicer than the beautiful cliques, but they reserved their close friendships for members of their own tribe.

"You aren't part of the popular group?" Peggy asked.

I grinned. "You need to have an eating disorder and be smaller than a size two to qualify for that set." Most of the mean girls spent their lunch hour pushing their salads around their plates and sipping their diet drinks."

"Poor things. Food is one of the great joys of life. They will never get to taste my Mom's fabulous home-baked, chocolate-chip shortbread cookies."

"Good thing I'm not anorexic," I hinted.

"Want to come over and study at my house tomorrow afternoon?" Peggy asked. "I'll check the cookie supply."

* * *

Peggy rapidly became my BFF. We studied together after school, usually at her house because mine, with two noisy younger siblings, was not conducive to concentration. The house was gorgeous, and Peggy's mother was warm and funny. Her reputation for making fabulous chocolate-chip cookies was well deserved.

We'd take walks in the Beverly Hills triangle, window shopping, since none of the stores sold clothes that would fit us. We'd stop for coffee at the Cheesecake Factory, and split a low- carb cheesecake, or meet for Sunday breakfast at Nate 'n Al's.

We made a daily habit of having lunch together at school, usually choosing a salad because, despite our mutual passion for good food, we were both constantly on a diet. Perhaps we imagined that our lives would be different if only we were thinner.

One afternoon, Peggy was particularly hungry, and filled her tray with a hamburger, piled high with condiments, and a chocolate milkshake. On her way to the table, she accidentally bumped into Jennifer, causing her to spill a Diet Coke. Peggy apologized, but Jennifer gave her a nasty look. That was the beginning of the disaster.

"Can you actually bite into that thing?" I asked. The burger was at least six inches thick.

Peggy grinned. "Let's see." She opened her mouth as wide as she could and took a bite. As she chewed both cheeks bulged. She washed it down with a sip of milkshake.

The next day, a video appeared on Jennifer's Facebook page, labeled "Piggy at the Trough" and showed Peggy demolishing the hamburger. The video drew vitriolic commentary from fellow students.

"Ugly Sow."
"Should be banned from the lunchroom."
"Watching her eat makes me nauseated."
"Gives new meaning to the obesity epidemic."

No need to go on. It wasn't long before an anonymous email informed Peggy of the Facebook post. When she didn't show up for lunch the next day, I found her in tears in the girls' bathroom.

"They're just a bunch of bitches," I said. "Tomorrow they'll find someone else to bully."

"At my other school they just ignored me," Peggy sobbed. "No one wanted to be my friend, but at least they didn't humiliate me."

"You're nicer and smarter than all of them," I drew her into a hug, but she couldn't stop crying.

I'd never liked Jennifer or any of her crowd. I'd viewed them with contempt for their nastiness and superficiality, but now, as I watched Peggy in tears, my contempt turned to fury.

Two weeks passed and I was increasingly worried about Peggy. We usually hung out together on Friday nights, but she said she didn't feel like it. I could tell she was depressed.

I'd expected the cyber bullying to stop by now, with Jennifer and her clique of mean girls turning their vitriol on someone else. Unfortunately, it evolved into face-to-face insults. Students she didn't even know called her *Piggy Peggy* in the hallways or oinked when they saw her in the cafeteria. After a day or two she began retreating to the school library during lunch hour.

I texted Peggy all weekend, but she didn't answer. On Monday, when she failed to show up at school, I called her mother.

"She's got a bad headache and is probably coming down with a cold," Peggy's mom told me. "I told her she didn't have to go to school today."

"Can I talk to her?"

"She's sleeping."

"Well, when she wakes up, just tell her I called and was worried about her. I'll be at home if she wants to call me."

Peggy didn't want to call me. My cell phone stayed silent all night. I decided that if she didn't show up at school the next day, I'd go over there. I was that worried.

Tuesday afternoon, as soon as school let out, I walked to the English Country house on Roxbury. Peggy's mother was in the driveway, unloading bags of groceries from the trunk of her SUV. I waved, and helped her carry them into the kitchen, where I put them on the huge island.

"Thank you, dear. Peggy is still under the weather. She's in her room, but I can't promise you won't catch her cold."

"I'll take my chances," I said.

"While you're going up, can you take her a cup of tea with honey and some cookies?"

I waited as Peggy's mom prepared a tray and I carried it up the wide staircase.

Peggy's room was a suite, with a sitting room, a spacious bedroom and a bath. It was practically an apartment, and I envied her the space. I knocked, heard no response, and entered the sitting room. The bedroom door was closed.

A white leather sofa dominated the room, brightened with plump turquoise pillows. A dark blue afghan was artfully draped over the sofa back. A beautiful glass vase full of dead tulips sat on a shiny wood coffee table.

Peggy loved flowers, and every time I'd been here, the vase was filled with fresh garden blooms. I still remembered the vibrant red tulips from two weeks ago, before the Facebook disaster. Now, there they sat, dead, neglected, waterless, a reflection perhaps of Peggy's mood. I wanted to cry. What could I do to comfort her? How could I make this better?

I knocked at the bedroom door, balancing the tray. Peggy didn't answer. After a few more knocks I tried the doorknob and it turned. I walked in.

The scene before me rendered my body frozen, my voice mute. The tray smashed to the floor, the cup shattered, and hot tea soaked into the carpet. I dropped to my knees, closing my eyes, willing the horror to disappear.

Peggy had rigged a noose out of a belt, looped it over her closet door. Her limp body hung lifeless, her face grotesquely swollen and blue. The desk chair on which she had stood was on its side. A note, in a flowered pink envelope, lay propped up on her desk, addressed to "Mom and Dad."

I have no idea how much time passed before I let out a desperate scream for help.

In the weeks after Peggy's suicide, I was devastated. I waited for justice to be done. Students were shocked that one of our classmates had died, but few of them had known Peggy or cared that she was gone. The school held a memorial service for her, but only a handful of students attended. Mrs. Schneider, our counselor, made herself available to students who were having trouble coping.

I made an appointment.

"Peggy killed herself because she was bullied to death online," I declared. Taking out my phone, I brandished Jennifer's Facebook post. "The bullying went on for weeks. What are you going to do about it?"

If I'd been the principal, Jennifer would have been expelled the next day, and the entire student body would have gotten a lecture about the dangers of bullying. I would have made it clear that what happened to Peggy was unacceptable, and that any student who bullied another would be expelled.

Unfortunately, I wasn't in charge. Mrs. Schneider promised to pass on my information to the administration. I don't know whether she followed through. I do know that absolutely nothing happened.

Jennifer and her crowd of mean girls continued to rule the school as they always had. When the college list came out, Jennifer had been accepted at a prestigious party school. Clearly her bullying hadn't affected her college admission. I did a slow burn every time I saw her and fantasized about calling her out in public. Of course, I never did. If I'd confronted her, I would have become the new target, and at seventeen, I lacked the courage. At thirty-two, at the beginning of a successful medical career, I now had both courage and power.

* * *

Two hours later I returned to room number three. A nurse had hung a small IV bag filled with the first dose of anti-viral medication, and the respiratory therapist had fitted Jennifer with a mask. Her oxygen level was holding steady at ninety-two percent and her respiratory rate had slowed from thirty to twenty-six. She stared at me with those big blue eyes.

"I remember you," I said. "We were at Beverly Hills High together. My name was Meredith Wiskowski."

Her face was expressionless, her voice barely audible through the mask. "Sorry, I'm afraid I don't remember you, doctor. It was a big school."

"Perhaps you remember my closest friend Peggy," I said. "You were responsible for her suicide, you know." I wondered if she could see the hatred in my eyes.

I'm not sure what I was expecting her to say, perhaps something like, "*Oh my God, that's haunted me for years. I should never have done that Facebook post. I was too immature to realize what an unforgiveable act it was. If only I could go back in time and undo it. I've felt guilty ever since it happened and have tried to make up for it by being as kind as I can to everyone.*"

Of course, that was my fantasy. In real life, narcissists never feel guilty for their crimes.

Her perfectly plucked eyebrows came together in a skeptical look. "Piggy Peggy? She was no great loss to our class." She paused to take a breath. "How dare you accuse me of having anything to do with a mentally ill person offing herself?"

I could feel my face flush with rage. "Your nasty Facebook post started a round of bullying that plunged her into a severe depression. Peggy was a nice person. She didn't deserve what you did to her. Didn't you have the slightest feeling of remorse when she died?"

A puff of humid breath fogged the interior of her mask. "If

Peggy couldn't handle a joke, she was obviously a loser, and I have no patience with losers." She paused for breath.

"If you were her friend, then you're clearly one too, despite the fancy M-D after your name. You think you're so important?"

She was coughing now. I didn't respond.

"I know people who really matter in this hospital, and I can't wait to tell them that one of their physicians practically accused me of murder." Her respiratory rate increased markedly after her long rant.

I was fuming. "You really haven't changed since high school. You've just become nastier and more self-centered."

Jennifer glared at me. As I held her stare, I glanced at the monitor again. Her blood pressure and heart rate had increased along with her respiration. After half a dozen quick breaths, she continued.

"You just wait. By the time I'm done with you, this hospital will fire you and you'll lose your license. No one talks to me that way." She started coughing uncontrollably.

I turned and left the room, fighting the urge to pull the oxygen tube off the cylinder.

During a break in the endless flow of patients, I Googled Jennifer. She didn't have a job, like a normal person, but spent her time being a fashion and design influencer. I checked her Facebook page and Twitter feed. No surprise, it was full of bitchy, snide comments about other women who didn't meet her criteria for wealth, beauty or anorexia. Her grandiosity rivaled that of Trump.

Worse, she was married to a wealthy, hot-shot producer who was on the board of directors at my hospital. He'd donated a wing and a research chair, and I'd seen his name in The *L.A. Times* as a major donor to multiple community hospitals and universities. I was truly in trouble. Once she complained to her husband, my medical career would be over. It was fortunate that Covid patients were not allowed to have visitors. Fighting a rising sense of panic, I deleted the search from my phone.

When I'd graduated from medical school, I'd taken the Hippocratic Oath to do no harm. Actually, doing harm had never occurred to me. I was in medicine because I wanted to care for people and make a difference. Each patient I cured, or helped, or freed from pain was one more brick in my wall of self-esteem. Being a doctor was my identity. It was my life, and Jennifer was threatening to take it all away. I wasn't naïve. If a multi-million-dollar donor asked the hospital's CEO to fire a doctor who had insulted his perfect wife, I didn't have a chance. Jennifer had destroyed Peggy's life and now she was about to destroy mine.

All my problems would disappear if Jennifer died from Covid, but I couldn't count on it. If she needed a respirator, no doubt they'd put her first in line. I couldn't ignore this. I had to do something to save myself, even if it meant breaking my oath. I could only think of one way to do damage that wouldn't lead back to me.

Making sure I was unseen, I slipped a 50cc syringe and a needle into the pocket of my white coat.

I checked Jennifer's vitals on the monitor at the nurses' station.

She'd gotten much worse while I'd been on Google. Her fever had spiked to one-hundred-four. Her oxygen saturation was eighty-eight percent, and she was breathing much too fast. As I opened her door, I could hear her gasp with each breath. Jennifer needed a respirator and an ICU bed.

"Help me," she whispered, turning her frightened blue eyes in my direction. I walked toward her. The nurse call-button was inches from her hand, lying on the bed. I pushed it out of her reach.

"It sounds as if you need a ventilator," I said. "I'll call the ICU."

Jennifer began to cough, horrible racking sounds, her face turning red with effort, her eyes shut tight.

I took the syringe out of my pocket, drew up 50cc of air, and reached for the IV port. An air embolism was a perfect murder weapon. Fast, lethal and untraceable. There would be no suspicion. People were dying of Covid-19 every day.

Could I really do it?

Her oxygen saturation continued to drop. I hesitated. *Shit.*

I stuck the syringe back into my pocket and reached for my phone to call the ICU. Jennifer arrested.

My brain went on auto pilot and I pushed the Code Blue button. I heard the blaring alarm, and the announcement "*Code Blue, Emergency Room, Exam Room Three. Code Blue, Emergency Room, Exam Room Three.*"

The person who pushes the button is required to start CPR immediately. Five minutes without oxygen and the brain turns into a vegetable. Unlike the medical dramas on TV, few people emerge unscathed after being resuscitated from a cardiac arrest. I doubted that Jennifer would. CPR consists of squeezing the heart under the sternum to get blood flowing and forcing air into the lungs. Unfortunately, we didn't have any airway equipment in the room. The only way to force air into Jennifer's lungs was via mouth-to-mouth. I removed the blanket, found a stool to stand on, and began doing chest compression. I drew the line at mouth-to mouth. There were patients I might risk my life for. Jennifer wasn't one of them.

The Code Blue team converged on Jennifer a few seconds later. I watched as they took over the CPR, intubating her, and shocking her heart to no avail. They kept trying for half an hour until the attending physician finally called the code.

My nemesis was dead.

I had no regrets for not doing everything I could have done for Jennifer, knowing, as I did, that even if the team had resuscitated her, she would have severe brain damage. Truth be told, I was glad she was dead. Covid had saved me from becoming a murderer and had avenged Peggy. I'd have many more years to practice medicine.

As I stood staring at Jennifer's lifeless body, I made a promise to myself. I'd be the best doctor I could be. I'd be kind to my patients, listen to them, and make sure I didn't miss anything when I made my diagnosis. I'd risk my own life, again and again, during this pandemic, and I would bend over backward to save every future Covid patient who came my way.

After all, saving lives is my job.

THE MAGIC HOUR

Peggy Rothschild

The house was quiet. Dirty dishes sat in the sink. The smell of spaghetti sauce hung in the air hours past dinner time. The source: a hardened splash of red paste decorating the counter. The pattern reminded her of the scattered freckles on the boy's nose and cheeks. Parting the kitchen curtains, she stared out into the side yard. The neighbor's security lights hadn't blinked off yet. She waited. Two minutes passed before the harsh bulbs went dark. Once night was restored, she looked up. Clouds hid the moon, but a narrow break revealed an inky sky. No stars. At least not that she could see. Light pollution concealed those brilliant bodies.

The neighborhood sat two miles north of LAX. Far enough away for people to enjoy their yard without smelling jet fuel. Far enough to sit on the porch and pronounce the night peaceful and quiet. Guests would nod in agreement, all of them city folk too long removed from what real quiet sounded like.

She walked across the kitchen, through the doorway into the living room, moving like a wraith. Parting the drapes there, she stared out. On the opposite side of the street, the two-story Cape Cod-style cottage had one light on upstairs. The *faux* adobe to its left sat in complete darkness. The snakelike street was transforming, shedding its old, tired skin. Convenient to

Silicon Beach tech companies, McMansions now replaced the three-bed, two-bath homes that had once sat behind patchy lawns. It hardly looked like the neighborhood she once knew. The place where she'd felt most at home.

But even with the changes, the area had remained safe, a place where people could forget to lock their doors, and everything would still be okay. She let the curtain fall back, comfortable in the shadows. Turning on a light might wake the children.

Carpet muffled her steps on the way to the stairs. Keeping her feet close to the wall, she crept upward. Though eager to see the children's sleeping faces, she forced herself to tread with care. If she woke them, the momentary peace would be ripped apart.

This was her favorite time of day. The magic hour when the clock hands met as if in prayer. Was it wrong that she found children easier to love when they were asleep? When the night gifted them with stillness, she saw perfection. Little people lost in big dreams. Sailing free. You could gaze at them and believe they were angels. Pretend they had no driving impulse to destroy.

If only they could stay that way.

The bedroom door creaked as she eased it open. She froze. The boy didn't stir. Slipping inside, she waited for her eyes to adjust to the deeper darkness. There he was: inky hair tufted against the white pillowcase, mouth slack, one hand curled beside his cheek. How different from this morning in the front yard, with his dramatic glances left and right. Then, once he thought no one was watching, taking aim. The dirt clod hitting his sister square in the back. The screaming that ensued. The tears. Little arms reaching up for comfort. No bandwidth left to deal with the boy arming himself and throwing again. More yelling.

She inhaled and tamped down the spurt of anger.

When her own children had been babies—her son toddling from room to room while her daughter crawled like a crazed bug—she'd felt on the edge of madness. Daily. The need for watchfulness tugged on her nerves until they practically vibrated. Constantly on alert, anticipating the next disaster. There was always a next disaster. Back then, naptime provided the lone slice of sanity.

She stepped closer to the boy's bed. Restless, he stirred but didn't wake.

The room smelled vaguely of graham crackers and apple juice. A snack left somewhere to spoil? She cast her gaze about, but the shadows kept their secrets. Children did, as well. It had taken too many years and tears before she'd grasped that children were anything but innocent.

Near the small desk, a Lego castle rose four feet in the air. Almost as tall as the boy. An action figure lay at the foot of the bed, one leg missing. Dirty clothes formed a tangled hillock in the corner and his small sneakers stuck halfway out from underneath the bed. Why hadn't he put the shoes in his closet? It was only a few feet away. Did he think monsters lived inside it? Many children did.

The only noise besides the boy's gentle snoring was the ticking of the wall clock, which was shaped like an airplane. She closed her eyes and took a deep breath, trying to record the details. This was what peace felt like. A rarity, it required deep appreciation. But calm as this moment was, it wouldn't last. She shouldn't linger.

Every mother knew: there was always more to do. Plus, she still had the little girl to tend to. Moving closer, she stretched out her hand. The boy's small chest rose and fell in time with her beating heart.

Melissa bolted upright, eyes wide. What had awakened her? Had one of the children cried out? She clutched the blanket's satin binding, listening.

Nothing. Nothing except her snoring husband. Oblivious as usual. She sniffed the air. No smoke. She cocked her head. No sirens. Still, maybe she should step into the hallway. Tim insisted they shut their bedroom door at night. Said they needed their private space. Right. For her the closed door meant she had to sleep lightly in case anything happened beyond it.

Hell, maybe it was one of Tim's juddering snores that woke her. Sometimes it sounded like the world was crashing to an ugly end when he slept.

Might as well check on the kids. Just in case.

Tim swore she coddled them. Maybe she did. But who else was going to take on that task? Not him. He snorted then mumbled and shook his head as if warding off unpleasantness.

She should wait. At least until he was sleeping deeply again. Otherwise, he'd startle awake at the squeak of the bedroom door. He always did. And then he'd chide her for worrying. If only he'd oiled those hinges like he promised. She bit back a sigh. He needed a good night's sleep. He had that important meeting tomorrow.

She was probably just wound up because of this morning's turmoil.

It was hardly the first time she'd sat staring into the darkness, worrying about her kids. She wished they got along better. Before Collette was born, she'd imagined their son proudly cuddling his baby sister, defending her against imagined threats. Wanting to play with her. Wanting to look after her. She wouldn't say Caden didn't like Collette. Not exactly. It was more like he was indifferent. But she also couldn't say he loved his sister. A familiar sadness pooled inside her.

She should go back to sleep. Creeping into Caden's room was sure to wake him. An anxious, fidgety sleeper, entering his room at night without disturbing him was nearly impossible. And if he woke, he'd make enough noise to wake his sister, too. He always did.

Maybe if everything remained peaceful for the next few minutes, she'd let herself close her eyes.

Her pulse jumped into her throat. There it was. Not a noise. Not really. More of a sense of movement. Was Caden out of bed?

She peeled back the covers, easing her weight off the mattress.

It was probably nothing. Like many nights before. She doubted she'd had a solid eight-hours' sleep since Caden was born. High energy. Short attention span. An ever-changing alphabet soup of diagnoses. No wonder her nerves were frayed.

Tim snorted and rolled onto his side. Melissa resisted the urge to nudge him and insist he join her vigil. No. He had a lot on his plate tomorrow.

On silent feet, she crossed the carpet, toes curling into the deep pile. Twisting the knob with care, she cracked the door. Placing her ear to the gap, she strained for any sound that shouldn't be there.

Still quiet. But...what was that? Her heart began to sprint. Something was off.

Wrong.

She raced to her husband's side of the bed and shook his shoulder. "Tim." Fear strangled her, turning her voice into a hiss. "Get up."

He threw an arm over his eyes.

"Wake up." She shook his shoulder again. "Now."

Tim lurched forward, eyes wide and confused. "What's going on? You okay?"

"Someone's inside the house."

A soft voice. Footsteps.

She froze.

Light seeped from the hallway into the boy's room. Next, an intense yellow beam burst through the door, which she'd left ajar. She jerked away from the bed, into the shadows. The bedroom door banged open.

A woman screamed, her anguished cry waking the boy.

Sleepy-eyed, he sat up. "Mommy?"

The ceiling light clicked on, blinding the intruder.

Then the father charged in, a raised baseball bat in his hand. "Get away from my son!"

The boy's mother dashed to the bed and snatched him up. Though far too big to carry, the woman cradled his pajama-clad form against her chest as if he were an infant, tears running down her face. "Oh God, it's that crazy lady from this morning. The one Caden threw dirt at."

"Call nine-one-one." The husband held out a cell phone to his wife, the other hand brandishing the bat.

"What's wrong with you?" the mother screeched to the other woman, clutching her son closer. "It was just some dirt."

"Melissa! Now!"

The mother took the phone, punching in numbers as she carried the whimpering boy from the room.

The father shifted his weight, bat aloft, ready to swing. "Drop the knife."

The broad silver blade gleamed in the overhead light. She stared at the empty bed. Everything was ruined. The boy was awake. Soon his sister would be, too. The magic hour had been destroyed.

If only she hadn't taken time to savor the moment. If only she'd acted. Done what needed to be done. Taught the child and his negligent mother a much-needed lesson. Then the boy and girl could have slept forever. Peace would have returned to the neighborhood.

Still clutching the knife, she lifted her gaze to meet the man's glowering eyes. "I love it when children sleep."

GUNNING FOR JUSTICE

Laurel Wetzork

February 25, 1942
Santa Monica, CA

Gladis hiccupped. It was two a.m. Quiet. No practice air-raid sirens so far. Slow-moving tendrils of fog glowed from the full moon. Palm trees loomed. The swish of the fronds in the foggy breeze whispered, "Be careful, shhhh." Her co-worker and friend Betty's second-floor apartment window was dark, but so was every other apartment window in this three-story building. Dark from blackout curtains. She refastened her garter and adjusted the small packet held there, pulled her skirt hem into place, smoothed the cuffs on her long-sleeved blouse, and slipped off her shoes. She examined the left shoe's loose heel, hoping it would stay on in case that dreaded Stairwell Killer the newspapers kept gabbling about leapt out and attacked. She'd whop him with the shoe.

Betty's apartment building had a well-lit stairwell beyond the blackout curtains, just like the other crime scenes. Those blackout curtains had hidden the murderer from street view. Three young women in the last two months. Frizzy hair, olive skin, short, and stocky. Just like her. The women had been violated and garroted in stairwells, then abandoned in alleys. Santa

49

Monica had lots of buildings with stairwells and plenty of alleys with hiding places. The killer might be close.

Gladis hiccupped again. Damn the bartender at the Caribbean Coastal Tiki Room. If his pour was a half-strength Martinique Crusta cocktail, a full-strength would have her seeing triple. The world was blurry enough now with the ghostlike fog.

Gladis tucked her right shoe into her purse and held up the left shoe in whopping position. She slipped in the main door and carefully navigated the wooden stairs, softly humming Glenn Miller's "A String of Pearls," pacing her tip-toe steps to its beat. She rounded the stairway curve and swayed to a stop. A strip of light gleamed from under Betty's door. Oopsie. Maybe Betty had a special friend visiting. Navy, Air Force, Army and Coast Guard. Betty didn't care which service, as long as their service satisfied her. Gladis frowned. It was crucial that she talk to Betty tonight—to get to the truth—regardless of whether Betty had a new soldier pal over. If she did, she needed to kick out whatever besotted tangle of manhood lay under equally tangled sheets.

Gladis quickly decided what she'd say: *Betty, I'm so sorry but 'slayer,' the bartender over at CC Tiki, splashed out one too many of the rum cocktails and the Red Line Cars don't run this late.* Correction: *run this early. And there was this guy, he got a bit—a bit rough.* There was always a guy who got a bit rough. *And I couldn't afford a taxi and there was no reliable way to get from Santa Monica to my folks' house in Pasadena this late, so could you please just let me sleep here, again? I swear it'll be the last time—please, please?* That should work.

She tiptoed to the door and listened. No noise. Not even Betty's snoring. Gladis reached up and felt atop the doorframe. There. She grabbed the key and let herself into the studio apartment.

The place smelled of Betty's perfume, Lanvin's Rumeur. A femme fatale perfume, dark, haunting and dangerous. It smelled of vanilla, musk, and florals. Not Betty at all. If Betty were bottled as perfume, the scent would be citrus, daisies, and freshly mown grass. It'd be sold as "Girl Next Door."

The kitchen light above the small sink toned the wall golden. The trundle bed was neat, the faded lace pillows in their usual place atop the homemade quilt. No lumps, therefore, no bodies under the covers. And trundle beds didn't have room underneath for bodies, anyway, so no need to check. Tiny dining table, spotless. A small tin can with a bedraggled daisy was centered on its Formica surface. Two chairs, hand-painted green and chipped in places, were tucked under the table. The bathroom's yellow tiles and green baseboard were visible through the open door. Gladis peered into the shower. No bodies there, either.

The typewriter atop the small desk in the corner was uncovered. A piece of paper sat in the carriage. Nothing unusual about that. Betty worked for the same rag she did, *Charming Women: for the glamorous hard-working gal!* What a load of hooey. Just short articles about time-saving kitchen devices, ways to improve the mind, and cheap fashions. Filler around the advertising, which, as far as she could see, separated the hard-working gal from any small amount of money she earned. Wait. Betty did all her typing at the office. She hurried to the typewriter and jerked out the paper.

"Gladis, if you drop in like usual, I'm going to take a flying horizontal dive at Joseph (upstairs)! If it's before four a.m., come up and softly tap seven times fast and two slow, and we'll know it's you. If we answer, my dive failed. If we don't, I'm busy, go away, and see you in the morning. Don't use all my sugar in the miserable drink you call coffee. I don't care what they say, I'm rationing now."

Gladis took a resentful breath. Her coffee wasn't miserable, just mud-like. She folded the paper. Well. Upstairs, huh? Betty had fallen into temptation after all. Still, they had to talk. Tomorrow might be too late. She hiccupped. Damn that bartender.

She slipped out of Betty's, restored the key, and, clutching her purse and readying her left shoe, tiptoed upstairs. The hair on her arms shot straight up. *Where does the Stairwell Killer hide? Stairwells. Well, I'm ready.*

Light shone from under Joseph's door. She didn't like Joseph. She could always use her shoe to whop him on the side of the head if he was taking advantage of Betty. She fingered the heel of her shoe until it clicked, took a deep breath, and tapped seven times fast and two times slow.

There was a muffled noise, then the door opened a crack. Joseph's blue eyes glinted down at her. His blond hair was tousled. He yanked her inside. The hairs on her arms didn't go down. He quickly shut the door behind her and locked it, blocking her view of the left side of the room. He smiled an oily, arrogant, and entitled smile. A rich boy's smile. He tugged one of her curls. She batted his hand away and peeked behind him. Was Betty there? Nope.

A large painting, a knock-off of abstract swirls, hung on the wall to her right. The painting's metallic frame was a torturous weave of wires. Several wires sprouted off the top and led around the upper edges of the ceiling. Interesting. She looked down. If the mauve carpet could speak it would scream at the green walls. The large daybed covering was a houndstooth pattern in black, deep blue, and orange. A headache flared in her right temple.

"It came furnished." Joseph hadn't moved. He smelled of Old Spice, macaroni salad, and rage. She leaned to her left. The kitchen and dining room were a mess, and there was Betty, strapped to a chair, a circle of wire around her neck, a gag in her mouth, and blood on her cheek.

Fear shot through Gladis. She swung her shoe. Joseph blocked it, grabbed her hand, and twisted it behind her back. He pulled her close. Her shoe dropped to the floor.

"Don't scream or I cut your friend."

"Your breath stinks of mayonnaise and I'm not into your type of kinky." Her voice shook.

"Quiet, or I use this wire." He dangled a circlet of garroting wire in front of her nose. It was a match for the wire about

Betty's neck. He frog-marched her over to the only other chair in the room, to the right of Betty's and up against the wall.

"Sit."

Gladis sat.

"Nice gams." He tied her legs to the chair, using a rope that was quarter-inch twisted and braided. It looked like cotton. He wrapped seven turns around her ankles.

She kept her knees clamped together as best she could. Couldn't trust this type not to feel up her thighs. He slid his hand up her calf and under her knee.

"Don't."

He chuckled. "I am not that type of kinky." He removed his hand.

Gladis calculated the angle needed to launch herself forward and hit his head with the top of her head. The angle wouldn't work, and she guessed that his skull was thick. She'd probably fall over and knock herself out on top of her dirty shoe. She stared at Betty. Betty's blond pin curls were barely mussed. The cut on her cheek wasn't deep. Her eyeliner was smudged but not as if she'd cried a bunch.

"Are you okay?" Stupid question; obviously, Betty wasn't okay.

"Mmmphpph." Betty struggled against her bonds. A tear rolled down her cheek. Gladis found it annoying that Betty could stay looking cute while tied up. Or detained. Or about to be garroted.

Joseph pulled her arms back and tied her wrists together.

"Let me go. I just came by to sleep—*hiccup*—to sleep over at Betty's."

"Quiet."

She took a deep breath and held it. Might also help stop the damn hiccups. He tied her to the chair back. Gladis fingered the cuffs on her sleeves, which she'd managed to pull down partway to protect her wrists. *At least they are out of view of this sadist.*

"I just have a few questions." He smiled his smug smile,

pulled out a handkerchief and dabbed it against the cut on Betty's cheek. "See? I am cleaning her face. It is not so deep." He examined the blood on the handkerchief and tucked it back into his pocket. He checked his watch. His eyes flicked to the wall painting. "Answer them and I won't hurt your friend."

"What kind of questions?" A flare of anger rushed up Gladis's gut.

"The kind you will answer, doll. Or I will pull this wire tight around Betty's throat and you'll watch her die."

"Die?" Gladis hiccupped. *So holding your breath doesn't work.* She looked into Betty's eyes. There was anguish, pain, and a deep layer of fear. Beneath that was a strange light—the light Betty had whenever she cheated at a game of gin rummy. Triumph.

Gladis turned away. A few of her own tears fell. *So is she my friend or not? Is she going to help? She's got the same tools I have, from our real boss. Why hasn't she used them? Too scared? No matter. I'd better think of a way out of here.*

"You're the Stairwell Killer!"

"Maybe. Maybe not." Joseph smiled. His teeth were entirely too white. "Betty isn't the 'type' of the others who've been found, is she?" he said.

"But I am?"

He reached out and yanked one of her frizzy curls.

"Maybe. Answer my questions and I'll let you both go."

"Don't hurt me," Gladis whimpered. She stared up at Joseph and blinked out more tears. His smile grew feral. *Good. He likes seeing me upset.* She breathed fast in and out. Her fingers worried busily at her cuffs. She looked past Joseph at the horrible reproduction and its wire frame. One wire followed the edge of the ceiling, then the corner of the room, then down into a black leather case, about the size of a typewriter case. Gladis swallowed an angry shout.

Joseph leaned close.

"Your friend Betty said that last night, over near Fort

McArthur, you two went dancing."

"She danced. I tend to stomp on people's feet."

"You met two soldiers. Betty's told me all about what one said."

Gladis swiveled her gaze to Betty. Sadness welled in her stomach. She looked up at Joseph.

Air-raid sirens wailed to life.

Joseph glanced at the windows. "Stupid. So many practice drills. But it will hide your screams." He grabbed her hair and yanked. "Talk."

"About what?"

"Their names, ranks, everything. They're from Fort McArthur. What do you know?"

"They were just guys I trampled! Their toes! I don't remember!"

"You do. Blond little Betty over there was apparently too drunk to remember."

Betty had pretended to be drunk to make soldiers talk. She did it for their real boss. To find out which soldiers spilled too many secrets. Which they reported back. Soldiers who blabbed were a danger.

She'd overheard their real boss late that afternoon, and then gone drinking to figure it out.

"...we've got a leak. And it's one of the girls." There weren't that many girls. Her stomach roiled. *Betty keeps making mistakes. But a traitor? I refuse to believe it.* Which was why she'd needed to talk to Betty's tonight—to make Betty tell her the truth. Sudden relief washed over her. *What a dolt! Of course! Betty's stalling, waiting for me to make the first move. She can't fight this guy on her own. Even though she has the same tools I do. Well, maybe not all.*

Joseph let go of her hair and walked to the window. He peered out. The small saw blade once hidden in her cuffs was now in her fingers. She worked away at the rope. The little blade slipped. *Dear heavens, please don't let me drop this like in*

all my practice sessions. Distract him. Keep his eyes on my face.
More tears fell, but they were real. Her wrists and legs ached,
and she'd just nicked her wrists with the jagged edge.

Joseph sauntered back. "No action on the streets. A drill. So
talk."

"Promise you won't hurt Betty?"

"I won't."

Gladis felt Betty relax just a hair.

The air-raid sirens continued.

"Those don't usually blast that long. Shouldn't you turn on a
radio and check?"

"I would know if it were real or not."

"You're a Nazi and the Stairwell Killer!"

"Perhaps. Perhaps I am just on the winning side. Soon-to-be-
winning side. It will be a wonderful melding of business and
government. Ford is already on our side. Politics don't matter
that much. Money, on the other hand...does." Joseph pulled
out a knife and cleaned his fingernails. "Go on, talk. Or I slice
both your cheeks. Then more."

Gladis bit her lip. He wasn't kidding. She hoped Betty was
ready. The cords were almost severed. *She must have cut her
own cords by now. Must be waiting for my signal.* Time to talk
and cover up any sounds.

"They, the soldiers, bragged about the tunnels. And the
spotters. And since the lumber freighter *Absaroka* was struck
off San Pedro on Christmas Eve, and then just a day ago—two
days ago since today's the twenty-fifth—the Ellwood oilfields
near Goleta were bombed, well, the soldiers talked about the
kind of guns they could use to defend us."

"What kind?"

"The Browning M2 heavy barrel air-cooled ground mounts.
And maybe the multiple machine gun mount M22 for two .50
caliber guns, mounted on half-tracks, a multiple gun motor
carriages M13 and M14. It depends on the model of half-track.
I think the M2 HB is better than the water-cooled antiaircraft

M2. The M2 HB weighs one hundred twenty-one pounds, the water-cooled weighs eighty-one pounds."

Joseph's blue eyes flickered with surprise. "You know weaponry."

"No, soldiers like to talk, and if I know what they know, they'll talk to me. But they usually only want to get to know me because they want to get to know Betty. So I memorize things." *Get to the packet in between my legs, and I'll have a chance. Blather on.* She hiccupped. "Like 'Both M2s have a cyclic rate of fire of four hundred fifty to six hundred rounds per minute, giving a muzzle velocity of two thousand, eight hundred—M1 ammunition—to two thousand, nine hundred—M2 ammunition f-p-s with a seven hundred and fifty grain, non-explosive—"

"All right. You seem to have a photographic memory. That is good." Joseph checked his wristwatch again. "How many?"

Gladis wiggled her legs. The packet was ready to grab. Her hands were free but holding on to the rope edges. *Now what? I need to create a distraction.*

"I think...I think—"

"Go on!"

"I think I'm going to be sick." Gladis leaned forward and aimed for Joseph's shoes. She made heaving noises. She managed a mouthful of spit.

"Verdammte Scheiße!" Joseph backed out of the way.

Gladis whipped her arms free, fumbled the .32 gun from her garter, and shot him. Twice. He collapsed. "That's for all the women you killed!" Blood spread out on the floor. She swallowed bile. *I've just killed a man and I'm going to faint.*

The air raid sirens continued to wail. She heard gunfire. She looked down at her gun. *No, not me.* This wasn't a test. This was real.

She cut off her leg bindings. The ropes dropped to the mauve carpet. She picked up her shoe, examined the heel, and set it atop the black case. She tucked the gun into her waistband.

Betty was crying real tears.

"Hang on." Gladis carefully removed the garroting wire, then took off the gag. She paused. Did she trust Betty? Yes. She'd have to give it her best. She cut Betty's bonds, helped her stand up.

"Are you okay?"

"I'm so happy you're here!" Betty hugged her tightly. "So sorry the shoe didn't work!"

"Its poison would have been quieter, but I'm not surprised he knew about it."

Anti-aircraft fire shook the walls.

"That's—that's an M2!" Betty moved back from Gladis. Her eyes flicked to the case on the floor, then to the blackout-curtained window. "I don't understand!"

"Come on!" Gladis turned off the light and they rushed to the window, pulled apart the dark fabric, and peered outside.

The fog was gone. The moon painted the palm trees with silver highlights.

Searchlights swept the sky. Shell bursts lit up the night. The ack-ack of machine-gun fire echoed down the street.

"Good heavens." A man and woman from the apartment building across the street ran outside and excitedly pointed upward.

"They left their lights on!"

"This is real, isn't it? An air raid, but by whom?" Betty pressed her lips together. Gladis pulled her close for a hug.

"They won't get us, don't worry. And we've caught a Nazi spy! Look, that case down there, it's a radio. That's why he was checking his watch all the time. You're crying. Come on, it will be okay. He tried to kill us. I'm sure he's also the Stairwell Killer!"

"He is." Betty shoved her away. "It's not that."

"What?" Her stomach roiled again.

"You just—you just killed him!" Betty stomped over to the black case.

Chills ran down Gladis's spine. The comforting weight of her

.32 was gone.

Betty continued. "And the big oaf had me gagged so I couldn't warn him. 'It'll look more real,' he said. I warned him!" Betty pointed Gladis's gun at Gladis. "Don't move. You know I can shoot. I've got to report in. The sub will dive soon."

Betty brushed Gladis's shoe aside, opened the case, and turned on a radio set. A German radio set. Betty adjusted the dial. The gun didn't waver. Static screeched forth, then a stream of agitated German.

"Submarine?" Gladis swallowed. Had war come to the U.S. already? "A German submarine? Germans attacking from the air, too?"

"Not the air raid, that's not us."

"*Us?*"

"Yes. Us, Germans. Whatever that is outside, it isn't us. We're aiming for Fort McArthur from the submarine. You have a photographic memory. You know the harbor defenses at Fort McArthur. So cough up the details. And, sorry, but I'll have to use the garrote on you."

Gladis cursed her own stupidity and naivete. She wanted a friend, and Betty had pretended to be one. "So, I'll be one of his victims. I see now why he chose my 'type!' He killed the others, to cover up my murder."

"You don't count. They don't count. I'll say I heard you struggle, came up here and shot him. Too late for you. God! It wasn't supposed to be like this!"

Gladis calculated the distance needed to tackle Betty.

"I loved him!" Betty's tears were real this time. "Get in the chair."

Gladis edged toward the chair.

The radio crackled. A surprised, German-accented voice broke through the static. "Wolf, calling wolf, are you there? Not in our plans!"

Betty wiped away her tears with the hand holding the gun and picked up the microphone. "Wolf's cub here, go ahead."

Gladis launched forward. Betty swung the pistol toward her. Time slowed.

Gladis knocked Betty's arm upward, tackled her, wrested the gun away. She grabbed her shoe and leapt backward. Her breath came in short gasps.

Betty slumped over and sobbed.

The voice on the radio continued. "—cancel—too much attention on coastal waters—not us attacking—"

"I'd like to shoot you." Gladis fingered the trigger, then slid the safety into place. "But I think the major would rather I brought you in. Along with that radio."

The Battle of Los Angeles, a real event, took place in the early morning hours of February 25, 1942. It began at two twenty-five a.m., when the U.S. Army announced the approach of hostile aircraft from the east, and the city's air-raid warning system went into action. Gun crews at army posts fired into the sky for hours. But there was no air raid and no enemy planes. It was all 'war nerves.' Several people died though, of heart attacks and auto accidents. Nineteen-pound anti-aircraft duds were dug up from the ground, including from streets in Santa Monica. There were also German spies who communicated with Germans via radio.

BEST SERVED COLD

Gay Toltl Kinman

Jane Drake stepped through the front door and surveyed the living room of the Beverly Hills penthouse she knew well. She left the door open a crack as she continued to look around. Cathedral ceiling with stained wooden beams, white carpeting, silk wallcovering and—

Richard Hollingbrooke.

She had other names for him, but no time for that now. She had thought and planned this day for a long time and was finally able to serve the dish cold.

"Janey-poo, so good to see you. Good timing. Mariah just left, and she's not going to be back for a while."

A long while for you, Richy-poo.

"Let me make a short phone call and then we can get down to pleasure." *A jackal smile.*

Jane almost gags at the thought of "pleasure" with him. That included drinks on the way to the bedroom. "Who are you calling, Richy, your latest girlfriend?" She knew he hated to be called *Richy*, but she wasn't going to goad him too much with that. At this point it was like driving a Mac truck over a flea.

"Janey-poo, how can you say that? I'm true-blue to Mariah, but she isn't here. It's just you and me. We'll have a great time."

Did he rub his hands with glee? *Of course.* Did he leer? *Yes.*

"Make your call, Richard." He would cancel out his girlfriend.

When he came back from his whispered, muffled phone conversation, Jane was standing in the same place by the door.

"Janey, make yourself comfortable. I'll get the champagne and then we can have some fun."

She almost laughed. "I've come to tell you in person. I'm changing publishers."

Richard stopped, still for a moment. Then he laughed. "You have a great sense of humor when you use it." He looked at her again. "You're not kidding?"

Jane shook her head.

"Why? I've given you the best deal of all of my authors. You're top of the line, you get the best covers, advertising—the best of everything. Why?"

"For what you did to me." She knew he'd be clueless. "Ten years ago," she added.

"I didn't know you ten...years...ago." He emphasized the last three words.

"If I had listened to you then, you wouldn't know me now." All of the venom that she had kept dormant through the years came out.

He shook his head slowly. "I don't remember ever meeting you."

"You did. Ten years ago, I was a new writer at a writers' conference. And you were the lauded critic. I paid a fee to have you critique three pages. Three pages. And you couldn't even do that."

"What writers' conference was it? I go to so many."

"And you've probably trashed a lot of other writers who don't have the guts to never give up, like me."

"Babe, I don't have any idea what you're talking about. Come on, let's sit down, have some champagne. I want to hear all about it."

"No, you don't want to hear all about it." She said the last with all the sarcasm she had pent up. "But I'm going to tell you—in detail."

"All right," Richard sighed with resignation. "Tell me, ten years ago..." He did a winding motion for her to continue.

But she paused, studying him for a moment. "I never realized this before. You are a frustrated writer. You can't do it and you don't want anyone else to do it. Yet, you're in the publishing business. Interesting."

"How can you say that? I don't have time to write. Someday when I have time, I'll knock off a bestseller. My head is full of ideas." He waved an arm around his head as though the ideas were swirling like gnats.

"Knock off a bestseller? You mean if I can do it, it can't be that hard? And you can do it better?"

He went on as though he hadn't heard her. "But right now, I'm too busy nurturing other writers. I have a stable full of them."

"Stable." Jane thought about the word for a minute. *Not anymore.*

"Only after they've made it. You've never nurtured someone from the very beginning. Nurtured. That is such an odd word for you to use."

"I still don't get what you're so miffed about. I've never seen you in this kind of mood before. Tell me in plain English."

"In plain English, ten years ago, you were supposed to critique three pages of my manuscript. When I sat down at the table it was obvious you hadn't read them. You barely read the first paragraph and threw the pages down. They slid off the table and I had to get down on my hands and knees to pick them up. 'That's trash. Take up another line of work,' you said. Then you called, 'Next.'"

"No, no, I wouldn't—"

"You were supposed to give me a half-hour of critique. You were supposed to have read it and thoughtfully made notes to tell me how to improve it. That was your obligation. You were being paid to do this, plus free airfare, hotel, food and whatever else the conference provided, because you were such an important man and could lend insight to beginning writers. Nurture. *Ha!* What you did was the exact opposite. You didn't fulfill your contract—which is typical of your sloppy methods. I won't even go into your egocentric strutting. Or that you practically start to unzip every time you see a female body. And if that humiliation wasn't enough, you came on to me at the cocktail party that night. You didn't even remember who I was or what you had done. I was just another prospect for your bed. That's the only stable you ever nurtured. You are the scummiest of men. Using your prestige as a publisher to come on to new writers. You—"

"I'm getting some champagne. Think you need it, Janey-poo."

Jane realized she was not serving her dish cold. She was serving it piping hot, and that was not how she'd planned it. She was grateful she had a moment to cool her anger. She'd been storing up these words for ten years, rehearsing them in her mind, never saying them out loud because the time was never right. Now the time was right, and she'd better be, also.

Richard stalked off to the kitchen. No maid or Mariah to call to bring it to him. She stayed where she was. He came back with the bottle and two flutes. "Come sit down."

She shook her head.

He set the flutes down on the glass counter next to where she stood, filled them and then put the bottle down. He handed her a flute. She shook her head again. "Then I'll have to drink it myself." He downed the one he had offered her, set the empty glass next to the bottle, and then ostentatiously sipped the other one. "Mmmm, very good. You don't know what you're missing."

"I know what I'm missing, and it's not that." She felt like spitting out the words. She had let him stir up all those emotions again. She chastised herself. But she was past that. Now she was back in control, ready to deliver her bottom line. It felt good to be able, finally, to get her revenge.

He moved from his lascivious approach, which even he realized was not working, to the cool negotiator that he prided himself on being. "Janey, Janey, I don't operate like that." He spread his hands in an open gesture.

Jane looked at the picture of innocence he was trying to portray with disgust. That feeling must have shown on her face because he took a step back instead of forward.

"Yeah?" Jane said. "What about Mariah? She's a wonderful writer. You haven't 'nurtured' her. You've subtly trashed her, just like you have the others. Only you can be more cruel to your own wife."

Richard just watched her, toying with the flute, slightly swirling the champagne. Jane knew he was trying to look non-chalant, as though he didn't have a care in the world and wasn't worried about what she was going to say next.

But she knew he was.

"She doesn't have the ability. Pedestrian writing. She'll never match your talent," he said.

"I think she will."

"Then get your own publishing house and do it." *Smirk.*

"That's exactly what I plan to do, Richard. How insightful of you." Her turn to smirk.

"So you can nurture low-rate writers. Make them into best-selling authors?"

"I might. I'm a bestseller, but you only took me on after I hit the charts the first time. That's how you get your *stable*. Once they've made it you can lure them away with a bigger advance, more perks. I wanted you to take me on."

"I want to take you on, too. I know you've been in love with me for years," Richard said, holding his half-finished flute out, offering her a drink from it. *Leering.*

She must have had such a look of distaste on her face that he swallowed the rest of the champagne himself. He eyed the half-filled bottle but didn't move toward it. She could tell he was wearying of this conversation—he wasn't in control.

"Thanks to your generous advances—always earned out I might add—I've bought stock in your publishing house."

"Good investment, Janey."

"And that's another thing. My name is Jane."

"Okay, okay, Jane. So what about the stock?"

Jane could tell he was a little anxious. "As they say in the biz, it's time to update your resume."

"Janey, Jane. What are you talking about? It's my business. I own it. You can't get rid of me if that's what you're saying."

"You and Mariah owned fifty-one percent of the company. Now I own fifty-one percent."

Richard guffawed, but it was tentative. "That doesn't add up."

"It does when you add my stock to Mariah's."

Now he blanched. "You bought stock from Mariah?"

Jane smiled. She made it a cold, calculating smile.

"But that's impossible. She wouldn't sell our stock to you. She wouldn't combine her stock with yours." He kept saying the words over and over, as though trying to comprehend the possibility.

"It's my company now, Richard. I hold the controlling interest, and you are out. Plus, we've hired a forensic accountant. She found a lot of interesting things and notified the I-R-S about your creative accounting. You've been siphoning off funds from the company for years, paying non-existent vendors, under-reporting royalties. The I-R-S considers corporate fraud and tax evasion quite illegal, *Richy*. You're looking at a long time in prison. And then when your *stable* of authors sue you—"

"No way. Wait until Mariah gets back and straightens you out."

"She's not coming back to you."

"What are you talking about? Why wouldn't she come back?"

Jane laughed, her turn to guffaw. "Because you are a male chauvinist pig, a cheat and a crook?"

"What?" Richard looked incredulous, his eyes widening. Jane knew he was not able to take this in, or even comprehend what a *male chauvinist pig* was.

"Let's just say she got a better offer."

"A better offer? How could that possibly be? She has everything with me. Just look at this penthouse. She would never give this up."

"She isn't. It's in her name. *You* did that so that no one could take away your abode—legally."

"What!" Richard backed up and fell onto a chair.

Jane gave him time to sort out the implications.

"Who's the better offer from? She's never had another man."

"That's true."

Richard looked at her. "So who is she leaving me for?"

"Me."

"You! What are you talking about?"

"She's in love with me and I'm in love with her. We both love the publishing business and decided we wanted to own one. So now we have each other and our business, and we are going to publish her book."

"She's written a book? When?"

"Usually while you were off with one of your girlfriends. You know—all those conventions you were supposed to be at. And sometimes you were. But you always had a roommate. She has plenty of proof of your infidelities to get a divorce quickly."

"You and Mariah? I can't believe she's a lesbian." He thought some more. "I can't believe it."

"Believe it. You're out, Richard."

"What's her book about?"

"Ever the publisher. It's about a controlling husband who won't let his wife write a book. And so she does it while he's out philandering, which he does frequently."

"I'm calling Mariah now. You're not getting away with this. I don't believe one word you've said." He pulled out his cell phone.

Jane opened the front door wider. Mariah was standing there—with two police officers.

"Mariah, Babe, so glad to see you. I was just calling you. Janey, here—"

"Pack a bag, Richard. Get out of my condo."

"No, no, Babe, you can't do this to me. "

"My name is Mariah, not Babe."

Richard looked at the two of them. They were holding hands. Jane could see comprehension slowly crossing his face. "All of this because I didn't give you an A on your stupid pages ten years ago?"

Jane nodded.

MANNY'S ANGEL

Jenny Carless

It had been a hell of a week: old acquaintances dying, an inexplicable parade of tarantulas through my house, and then I saw Manny Peña lounging in the sun outside the Starbucks in Old Town Pasadena—just as if he hadn't been burned alive back in 1994, after all.

Spiders always made me remember Manny—and what happened that winter—so he'd already been creeping around the periphery of my mind. It's what helped me convince myself, that first time I saw him, that my mind was playing tricks on me. Still, I slumped down into a nearby patio chair and focused on remembering how to breathe until my body stopped shaking. By the time I pulled myself together and looked up across the street again, he'd gone.

The Northridge earthquake of 1994 conjured similar memories for everyone in the Los Angeles area: the dozens of deaths, the collapsed buildings and freeway interchanges, the gridlocked commutes for months afterward. People don't remember the fires and explosions—in trailer parks and other pockets around the city—as much. They didn't make the headlines because they weren't as widespread. For me, though, one trailer park fire remains seared in my mind—not only for the young man who died in it that morning but for what had happened to him several days earlier, deep in Monrovia Canyon Park.

1993

My friend Maria and I found our senior year at Azusa High School excruciating. Except for conservation biology, our classes bored us, and as a couple of shy, introverted girls, the social scene overwhelmed us.

We found comfort in each other's awkward companionship and disappeared into the woods of Monrovia Canyon Park, not far from our homes, whenever we could. Most park visitors hiked to and from the main waterfall, so we avoided people by taking other trails. During the winter 1993 school break, we spent most of our time off-trail exploring. The grandiose canopy of oaks, maples and sycamores, and the tall grasses carpeting occasional meadows made up for the damp, bone-chilling weather. These daily forays satisfied our appreciation for nature while giving us the escape we desperately needed from the social challenges of our school days.

So we didn't know what to make of it one gray afternoon when E and Cole showed up, tramping down the hillside toward us. E had thick brown, wavy hair and heavy eyebrows that, together with his deep-set, dark eyes, gave him a brooding, menacing look. He rarely smiled—but I soon learned that it was more affectation than anything else. I think even E saw himself for the cliché he was: a bored, rich kid looking for kicks.

Both towered over us at well over six feet. Cole was less imposing, though—partly because his red hair and freckled face just made you smile, partly because his body hadn't filled out yet to match its height, so he was all skinny arms and legs.

Equally wary of and intrigued by the two rich boys from San Marino who took an unexpected interest in our company, we fell for their flirting—at first. But the appeal, especially E's dark eccentricities, wore off quickly for me. I often wonder how my life would have been different if I'd been able to persuade Maria in those first few days to stop going to the park.

2020

Tuesday—two days after seeing Manny in front of Starbucks— was the fifth morning of the tarantula incursion. Before I'd even had a chance to dose myself with caffeine, I had trapped two of the hairy invaders under Tupperware containers on the kitchen floor—weighed down with cans of Campbell's tomato soup after the first one had lifted the plastic dome and crept out. The unnerving, persistent tap-tapping of those legs against the plastic made me shudder as I remembered a small shed in the forest and the cold January days of 1994. It took a full hour for me to get up the nerve to slide cardboard underneath each container and throw the tarantulas outside.

In the end, I skipped coffee and went straight for the Sangiovese I'd been saving for Jonathan's return. Glass at my side, I searched online for any evidence of some mass tarantula resettlement in Pasadena. Nothing. All I could fathom was that a neighbor must have released some "pets." My first thought was the neo-hippy family who had moved in across our back fence a month or so ago; I made a mental note to go and ask them. Whatever the reason, I'd reached the point where, if I had many more such mornings before Jonathan returned from his business trip, I'd be moving into a hotel—screw the mounting pile of bills on our kitchen counter.

And it wasn't just the tarantulas. Later that morning, I heard about E—on the radio just as I pulled into the Sprouts parking lot off East Main. While he hadn't lived in the L.A. area since high school, he often made the national news because he'd become famous over the years.

E died in a home burglary that had gone wrong, the newscaster said.

His face appeared to me as clearly as if I could reach out and touch it. The shock made my chest ache, and I felt like I was deep underwater, my lungs crying for air. I rolled down the window, leaned over and inhaled the searing summer heat—which didn't help much. My eyes burned as sharply as my lungs, and I leaned back against the headrest, eyes closed, trying not to think about E. Eventually, my breathing came easier, and I wiped my face with shaky hands.

The specter of those dark eyes wouldn't evaporate—but the initial shock finally dissipated and in its place rushed, surprisingly, a relief so strong that I almost laughed. It hit me then that I'd spent half my time that winter, and ever since, really, being afraid of E. Now I'd never have to worry about him again. Even better: Now one less person knew our secret.

I rested in the car for a while, eyes closed, listening to the sounds around me—a car door slamming, a shopping trolley squeaking by, a baby giggling—and letting the realization that E was really gone comfort me. When I eventually sat up straight again and opened my eyes, I reached for my water bottle but dropped it immediately. Right in front of me, beyond the car I'd pulled up behind, was an old Ford Falcon—just like the one Manny used to drive—cruising by. And guess who was driving?

Was it really him, or was it the news of E's death that had conjured up Manny in my mind? I didn't believe in ghosts, but I found myself struggling to explain how someone who looked so much like Manny had suddenly appeared in town—right when I was dealing with a tarantula invasion and had learned of E's death.

1993

The first day we met E and Cole, early in our winter break, we heard their deep voices and boisterous laughter well before we saw them. My mother's admonition against wandering alone in the mountains—that if we ran into some lunatic, no one would hear us call for help—flashed through my mind. Before we could decide what to do, the two of them appeared about fifty yards in front of us. Maria and I looked at each other, and in silent agreement, held our ground. Turns out we should have run.

We had come from two different worlds, not just two different zip codes. San Marino, their town, was multi-million-dollar mansions and The Huntington. Azusa, ours, was modest homes and a Superfund site. I imagined them being driven by chauffeurs through neighborhoods of manicured lawns, whereas Maria and I bicycled anywhere we needed to go—past fading multi-family buildings and industrial areas that we knew to avoid at night. E and Cole would go off to Ivy League schools later that year; whereas Maria and I had only just scraped together enough scholarship money to go to state universities.

We began to meet regularly in that same area, deep within the park. Within days, I hated it. E was edgy and unpredictable, and although Cole was kind and gentle with me when we were alone, it bothered me that he let E bully him into doing things he didn't seem to want to do. E bullied us both into doing things we should have just gotten to on our own. But I didn't see a way out without losing Maria's friendship and Cole's attention—or worse, *attracting* E's attention. If I'd been stronger—or braver—maybe I'd have walked away.

The four of us ran into Manny one day when he was out in the woods taking photos. He was a year behind Maria and me at Azusa High, and I knew him by sight but had never spoken to him.

The five of us walked through an oak grove together—Manny a little ahead of the rest of us. When Manny's cry broke through the woodland silence, it sounded more like a wounded animal than a human. I looked up to see him clawing the air in front of him and swatting at his face.

I hurried to him. "What is it?"

"N-nothing," he said. "Just a spider web." He tried to laugh, but his pale and sweaty face gave him away. I noticed a large spider scurrying across the path, away from his feet.

"Awww," E yelled, mocking Manny. His voice made me shudder. He zeroed in on Manny's obvious fear like an eagle clocking a rabbit. Catching up to Manny, he reached down, picked up the errant spider and tossed it in Manny's face. This time, Manny full-on shrieked.

E picked the spider up again, but this time he turned to me, his eyes locked on mine.

"Huh," I said, shrugging my shoulders. I clenched my jaw and willed myself not to react, knowing what it would cost me for E to see any weakness. Still, I felt sure that they had all seen the fear in my eyes.

Lucky for me, that day E seemed focused on persecuting Manny, and I got a pass. A few minutes later, when Manny didn't realize that E still had the spider, he snuck up on Manny and dropped it down his shirt. Poor Manny screamed out again and ripped his shirt off over his head, spinning around and scratching at his back until he saw the spider on the ground. At that, he ran ahead. Apparently finished with his cruel streak for the day, E let him go.

I remember locking eyes with Cole and seeing a peculiar expression on his face. He seemed to want to do something— but he didn't. Turned out he was just as afraid to say no to E as Maria and I were. Cole, who blushed when he kissed me and brought me straggly bouquets of forest greens when the others weren't around, seemed to know better than to push back against E.

E couldn't stop talking about Manny after that. He'd sensed vulnerability, it seemed, and became obsessed.

2020

Maria died in a single-vehicle accident.

Feeling groggy and hungover, I struggled to take in this news on Thursday morning. We'd all agreed to never see one another again after the incident, and it had been easy with E—even Cole. But I'd missed Maria. After years on the East Coast, I'd come back home to L.A.—Pasadena now, instead of Azusa— and Maria had eventually settled in Monterey. She became a well-known marine biologist, so I'd see her on the news from time to time. It didn't make up for our lost friendship, but nevertheless, I felt some kind of connection. Even though I hadn't participated in anything that winter, I'd seen it all, and that was bad enough. It was a lot to carry, and I'd always felt that if the day ever came when I just couldn't live with it anymore, she was there, just a day's drive away—one of only four people alive who could talk to me about that winter. Well, now only two.

The newspaper mentioned suspicious circumstances: Maria apparently had taken a freeway exit much too fast and lost control. No alcohol or drugs in her system, so the police launched an investigation. They asked for help from anyone who knew her "to get a better picture of her mental state." I had some ideas—but I knew I'd never make that call.

First E, then Maria. No one else would make the connection, but I started to feel hit on all sides: the spiders, these deaths, Manny's ghost. I wondered for a minute if I should contact Cole. He'd joined the police, of all things, somewhere in Colorado. I'd finally stopped monitoring him about five years ago, but it wouldn't be hard to find him again.

I realized quickly, though, that it would be a bad idea. Even after E's and Maria's deaths, the same reasons we'd stopped seeing each other—to hide our connections to Manny— remained just as valid. I just had to deal with this—whatever it was—by myself.

Later that day, I saw Manny—or his ghost—again, this time from my table on the small patio in front of Le Pain Quotidien. I must have been lost in thought—I'd had to deal with another monster spider that morning—when I looked across West

Colorado and saw him, once again, in front of Starbucks.

He leaned against the windows, one knee bent up, his foot resting against the low brick façade. He wore a cowboy hat and held a cigarette in his hand. He looked straight at me. In fact, he must have been waiting for me to look up, because as soon as I saw him—obvious because I spilled my coffee—he walked away.

Was I losing my mind? Did Manny have a doppelganger, or was it really his ghost? Whoever or whatever it was: What did he want?

I couldn't call Jonathan—I'd never told him anything about that winter. I couldn't tell anyone. I fumbled to clean up my spilled coffee and hurried away, watching out for Manny as I stumbled back to my car. I dropped the keys on the floor twice before managing to turn on the ignition, then squealed out of my parking space, forgetting all about the errands I'd planned to complete in and around Old Town.

1994

Maria's light brown pixie cut always made her look younger than she was—and the fact that she just reached five feet didn't help. But she looked old when she picked me up one foggy morning in Cole's car. Not college-age old, but world-weary old. She wouldn't say anything at first and barely looked at me.

"Where are we going?" I asked again as got out of the car in the neighborhood near the park entrance.

She just walked—past the entrance and then deeper into the park.

I heard shouting and crying before we crested the hill leading to one of our hang-outs—an old burned-out oak. Looking down, I saw E and Cole with a naked boy whose wrists were tied to one end of a long rope that had been thrown up over a thick branch of the tree. The boy looked a couple of years younger than the rest of us, and E and Cole were hoisting his skinny body by pulling on the rope. His howling was what I'd heard as Maria and I had approached. I could have told him his cries for help were useless; we never saw other people this far off the main trails.

"Stop it!" I yelled.

Cole gave me a nervous look and then turned back to E, waiting for instructions. I dropped to the ground and couldn't move. I didn't—couldn't—even look at the boy's face.

"Come over here and help," E called, his voice needling, cajoling.

I continued to stare at the ground in front of me. I wanted to do something, but I simply couldn't stand up to E—and I didn't want it to be me hanging from that tree.

Eventually, he stopped asking. He jerked and jumped around, his hands twitching, and he chattered incoherently—like how you see it portrayed on TV when someone is high on meth.

Later, the boy hung by his wrists, limp, dangling just an inch off the ground. There was no blood, no movement, no sound. Early on, E had stuffed something into the boy's mouth to muffle the howling, and the boy had finally stopped crying, too. He just stared off into the hills over our heads. They hadn't hurt him badly in a physical sense—but psychologically, I imagined that was another thing altogether.

2020

I wandered around in a stupor after hearing about Maria's death and seeing Manny's ghost again. I think I spent most of the afternoon on a chaise longue in the garden. I'd found the back door to the kitchen open when I got home, which gave me a whole new set of things to worry about. Was that how the spiders were getting in? Had I left it open in my frazzled state of mind? Had someone broken in? Were those weird neighbors putting the spiders in my house intentionally? We'd argued about the fence, I remembered, but it hadn't seemed like a big deal at the time.

Then, another night, another tarantula. I went to bed early but found one of the hairy critters under my duvet, so I decamped to the living room and made a bed on the couch—after pulling out all the pillows and shaking them, checking all around the sofa and shaking out the blankets.

The next morning, I felt better, knowing that I'd made it through the last night on my own. Jonathan would be home tonight, at last! Buoyed by the thought, I managed to start the day with coffee instead of Sangiovese. But when I looked at my phone, I saw that I'd slept through a call from Jonathan. His message said that he was having car trouble in Las Vegas and that he'd be gone at least another night, maybe two—some weird issue that the mechanic couldn't diagnose.

I just kept seeing the tarantula on my sheets. I imagined waking up the next night, feeling one crawling on me. That was it: I decided to find an inexpensive motel until Jonathan got back.

And I couldn't stop thinking about Manny. How could he be here, wandering around town like the living dead? Could he have faked his own death? Maybe it wasn't even that sinister. I remembered hearing that the authorities had been overwhelmed during and after the earthquake—they'd made mistakes, declared people dead who showed up a few days later. Maybe in Manny's case it was a mistaken identification or mixed-up paperwork.

But I also remembered the rumors—that after being released from the hospital he wouldn't leave his house, that he locked himself in his room when the fire came through his trailer park and died right there in his home.

I came to the conclusion that Manny must be alive. Just as I came to realize that the tarantulas in my house were no freak infestation. Sure, I was in a shaken mental state—but I was obsessive about locking doors. Just ask Jonathan. That led to some uncomfortable questions: How had Manny found me? How long had he been watching me? How long had he been breaking in? Did he know that Jonathan was away? Was I safe, even if I went to a motel? What was his end game?

In the middle of packing, I got a call from Seth Johnson, a journalist who was researching a story about Maria because of the unusual circumstances of her death. He'd been looking at old Azusa High yearbooks and wanted to talk to some of her school friends. I didn't want to talk to him. I tried to tell him that I really didn't know her that well, but I *did* want to know about how she'd died—whether it was an accident. He told me he'd share that information with me if I'd talk to him about high school. Even if I didn't know Maria well, he said, I could just tell him about what school had been like during our time. I said I'd think about it and asked him to call back later.

I decided to check the internet again. At this point, I knew it was just a matter of time until I found the news I was looking for. I drove to the library again—I'd become paranoid about doing research from my own phone or laptop, just in case someone was monitoring me. I'd even started wiping the keyboard down at the library after I used it. And of course, I found it.

Cole had died in the line of duty. Someone just walked up to his car and shot him in the chest while he sat in his police vehicle, waiting for his partner to come out of a store. So that was everyone—except me.

Even though I'd been expecting to find the news about Cole, my body erupted in a hot flash. My T-shirt clung to my stomach and back as sweat covered me from my scalp to the soles of my feet. Grateful that no one was using the computers next to me to witness my mini meltdown, I pulled off my sweater and flapped my arms to try to cool down. Eventually, I could feel the library's air conditioning again, and I pulled my sweater up over my shoulders before turning my attention back to my internet search. But I couldn't find any more information on Cole's, E's or Maria's deaths.

My one chance seemed to be Seth Johnson, so I Googled him. I found a website with links to lots of stories, mostly from publications I hadn't heard of, but he seemed legitimate. When he called back, I agreed to meet him that afternoon before checking into the motel.

Seth might be able to give me some more details about Maria's "accident," but he couldn't help me with the other questions churning in my mind: Why had I been left alive? Manny (or his ghost) clearly wanted me to see him—but he hadn't tried to kill me. Maybe in my case, I thought, he'd decided that the spiders were enough—just teaching me a lesson. Because I wasn't like the others.

A little part of me felt like I deserved it. Over the years, the times when I'd felt really down about everything, I wondered if I should have said something—to the police, to someone—at least after the fact. But what good would that have done? And I didn't think I could have made the others stop. Then after what they did to Manny, it was too late.

1994

A few days before the earthquake, E told us to meet him at our old shed. I had avoided everyone for a few days after what they'd done to the boy. But this wasn't just a friendly request from E.

The shed was old and ramshackle, no bigger than a small outhouse. We figured that it must have been used by the rangers at some point to store equipment. We'd been using it to stash some blankets and things. It was deep into the park, where we never saw anyone else.

When we arrived, I saw E standing there with Manny, who looked about to throw up. A cardboard box, about the size that could hold a basketball, sat on the ground next to them.

Manny had blood on his shirt. E held a knife casually in his right hand, his left latched hard onto Manny's arm.

"Open the door," E said to Manny, nodding to the shed.

Manny looked at us, clearly hoping for help. I looked at the ground.

"Open it!" E's voice echoed through the surrounding sycamores.

Manny inched over toward the door. I remember hoping that he wasn't claustrophobic, because we could all see what E had in mind. I also remember being so grateful, once again, that E wasn't picking on me. That gratitude sat uneasily with the guilt of not helping Manny.

Once Manny opened the door, E told him to get in, but he wouldn't.

"Get him in there," E growled.

He didn't need to ask twice. As Cole and Maria grabbed Manny by his arms, I inched farther away. Manny struggled, but they maneuvered him to the door, at which point Cole pushed him hard. Manny banged his head against the back wall, so it took him a few seconds to steady himself and turn around—enough time for E to pick up the box and pull it open. For an instant, I saw a writhing jumble of spiders as E threw it into the shed and slammed the door shut.

I heard Manny's screams in my ears long after I'd run far enough away to be out of earshot. I ran until my sides felt like E had stabbed *me*.

I never saw the others again. Maria and I avoided each other completely at school, and we never went back out into the canyon. We spoke just once more, on the phone, when she told me that they'd let Manny out after about an hour. She wouldn't describe what he was like, but I heard from someone else that he ended up in the hospital.

And then, just days later, the Northridge earthquake generated a magnitude six-point-seven earthquake. Burst utility pipes caused several deadly localized fires, and several people didn't make it out of their homes alive—among them, Manny. Or so I'd always believed.

2020

The afternoon had cooled but sweat trickled down my back as I walked through the wrought-iron gate, down the path toward the little restaurant Seth Johnson had chosen. I'd never been there before—the gate had always been locked when I walked by. Inside, it looked more like Big Sur than L.A. Rough wood covered the walls. Neglected hanging plants drooped from glass vases in wrought-iron frames. Indian-print tablecloths and bright-colored candles covered the fifteen or so tables crowded together in the small space.

A young woman hurried over when I walked in. She led me to a table against the far wall. She gave me a strange, almost suggestive, smile and left before I had a chance to ask for a glass of wine. The one I'd had at home hadn't taken the edge off. I took a slice of warm sourdough from the basket she'd left on the table and started pulling it apart. I looked around. The place was empty.

I wondered what Seth would be able to tell me about Maria—if there were any clues that would help me link her car crash to Manny, for example. I was about to get up and ask for my wine when I heard the front door bang shut. I turned around and saw Manny—or his ghost—standing by the door, holding a cardboard box. He locked the door behind him.

I looked around for the young woman.

"They've all gone," he said as he approached me. He smiled. "I told them it was our anniversary and that we wanted the place to ourselves."

That explained the woman's suggestive look.

Manny dangled the keys in his hand. "I told them I'd lock up."

I swallowed. Seeing him in front of me didn't make sense. "Is it really you?" I managed.

My question hung in the air, and suddenly I thought, *Maybe the spiders weren't enough. E, Cole, Maria…Jonathan's strange car trouble.* A burning sensation crept up my throat. I tried to push my chair back, but it was wedged against the wall. I tried to make myself smaller, cringed against the rough wood boards.

He didn't answer my question, but he pulled out the chair next to me and sat down, putting his box on the floor. It was the first time I'd had a close look at this man since the whole thing had started. It's hard to imagine how someone might change over the decades, and while I couldn't deny the resemblance, now that I sat right across from him, I couldn't be sure it was Manny.

I thought about running, but—just like all those times with E—I knew I couldn't get away.

"I thought you were dead."

Then it hit me. The shock of seeing him had thrown me, and only then did I wonder, *Where was Seth Johnson? And how did Manny know we were meeting here?* I was afraid to ask, but since he wasn't saying anything...

"I'm supposed to be meeting a journalist..." It also dawned on me that I wasn't going to get any answers about Maria.

My stomach tightened as he reached into his pocket. I half expected him to pull out a gun or a knife. But he slapped a driver's license down on the table in front of me. I slid it over toward me: Ángel Peña.

"Pretty slow, aren't you?" he said. "There's no Seth Johnson. I wanted to talk to you—to see you again."

"Peña. You're...Manny's *brother?* I never knew he had one." Now it made sense: the look-alike but not-quite-look-alike thing. But it didn't answer why he wanted to see me. And he thought we'd met before. "Were you at school with us?"

"Yes, but that's not what I'm talking about. You know your good friend E took a special interest in my brother."

"He wasn't a good friend." I felt my face grow hot. I didn't like the direction the conversation was heading. What did Ángel know? Did he think I'd hurt Manny? I had to make sure he knew that I hadn't.

"You were different from the others," he said.

I let out the breath I hadn't realized I was holding. Thank goodness. Manny must have told him that I didn't do any of those awful things.

"You're right, Ángel—and I've always felt terrible about what they did to Manny," I rushed to say. "But—I never helped them."

"You didn't try to stop them, either—and not just what they did to Manny."

What was he talking about? I thought about the other things E, Cole and Maria had done...*oh, no. The young kid!*

"You still don't recognize me?" Manny's voice grew loud. "Take a close look!" He leaned over and grabbed my face with a strong hand, forcing me to stare at him. Then he whispered, "You ran away while I was still hanging from the tree."

Tears spilled down my cheeks as Ángel pushed my face away. My neck snapped back, and I banged my head against the wall. It took a minute for the cloud of pain to dissipate.

"But .. but you said yourself, I didn't—" I left the thought hanging, crying silently.

Ángel stood up and towered over me. "You think you're less guilty because you didn't actually commit the violence? You're *more* guilty, because you could have tried to stop it, but you didn't. My brother was so traumatized that he just sat in our house and let it burn down around him. My aunt and I couldn't get him to leave. That's what your 'I didn't do anything' accomplished!"

Ángel and I were both shaking now. I leaned back against the wall, uselessly trying to put some space between us.

He leaned over me and whispered, "You of all people should have known what would happen to him after being locked in that shed. Manny told me that he'd seen the same fear in your eyes the first time E threw a spider at him."

He leaned down, picked up the cardboard box—about the size that could hold a basketball—and placed it on the table in front of me. In the silence, beyond the rapid thud of my heart, I heard light tapping and scratching against the inside of the box. I scooted my chair furiously to the side, but Ángel caught it with his foot. Bile erupted in my throat, and I felt a warmth spreading on the chair where I sat. I was too terrified to feel embarrassed.

"I have some friends I'd like you to spend some time with." He let that sink in. "You've met several of them already, at your house." He clasped my forearm with one hand, picked up the box in his other, yanked me out of my seat and said, "Did you know that old shed in the park is still there after all these years?"

AVENGING SUPERHEROES

Meredith Taylor

Nancy came into the kitchen and linked her arms around her mother's waist.

"Mo-om, can I give Wondrous Woman a cookie?"

Rachel Rogers smiled. *You never know what a kid will say.* She decided the pots soaking in the sink would do nicely and turned around to hug her seven-year-old daughter, then bent to look her in the eye.

She's so different from those big brothers of hers.

"Sure, Wondrous Woman can have a cookie. Why were you thinking about her?"

"She came to my room last night and we talked. She's really nice. She said she likes oatmeal cookies."

Of course, a female superhero, no doubt a member of the Avenging Superheroes, would like the cookies that were the closest to being good for you. Probably.

"Is she your new imaginary friend?"

Nancy tilted her head and looked into space for a moment. "I don't think so. Irene is my imaginary friend, and she might not like it if I got another one. Wondrous Woman is a person."

What in the world am I supposed to do with that?

"Come into the living room with me, hon."

Rachel and her daughter sat on the couch. Rachel held both

of Nancy's hands.

"Now, you know that Wondrous Woman is a lady in comic books and in the movies, right?

"Yes," Nancy said, nodding.

"And in the movies, she's a character played by an actress, who's very pretty and very nice, right?"

Nancy nodded again.

"So you understand Wondrous Woman is imaginary, right?"

Nancy squinted her eyes. "I know, Mommy. But she's also a nice lady who came into my room last night and said that I was brave and smart."

Rachel mentally threw up her hands. "At least she likes oatmeal cookies."

"That's right." Nancy smiled. "But she wasn't greedy. I asked her about cookies. She didn't ask me."

"I'm glad she was polite. Are the Avenging Superheroes always polite?" Rachel knew nothing about her sons' favorite comic book characters. But polite wasn't how she'd describe someone who enjoyed blasting bad guys and blowing up things.

Nancy thought for a moment. "I don't think Wondrous Woman hangs out with the Avenging Supers. I'll have to ask Greg or Jimmy for sure."

Rachel frowned. *Why ask Greg? Much too complicated. Why did it matter?*

"The boy heroes usually smash things," Nancy explained. "The girls are polite and sometimes they zap people. But only bad people."

Well, it could be worse. "You remember to be polite, too. With teachers and your friends—it helps." Rachel kissed her daughter and sent her outside to play.

A few minutes later, she stepped onto the patio to water her plants. It was a beautiful Pasadena afternoon, with vivid blue skies and a trace of clouds. Every so often Rachel enjoyed posting on Facebook: "Nobody has better weather today. Because there isn't better weather."

Facebook posts were for good stuff and happy events like birthdays. It was no place for subtle things or problems. She would never mention her troubles about her husband online. Worry was weighing her down. Tom was growing more and more withdrawn.

Lately, he was home on time, even early. At first, she thought he'd come up with a new plan: bring work home, finish it in his den, then come out to do more things with the family. A wonderful idea.

If that was the plan, it had failed. They still saw very little of him. He spent hours on the computer, locked away in his den.

Two days ago, he'd walked into the living room, his face as white as a stick of chalk.

When Rachel asked him what was wrong, his response had shocked her. "Nothing," he snapped. "None of your business."

Now in bed at night he turned away from her. There were no kisses or cuddles. This was not the man she had married sixteen years ago. Even though she was exhausted, she lay awake nearly every night, worrying.

That night, a slim figure tested a drainpipe on the outside of the house, then climbed lithely up it. On the second floor of the neatly painted Cape Cod cottage, a window had been left open to catch the cool Southern California air.

She pushed up the sash and climbed carefully into the upstairs bedroom.

Nancy sat up in bed. "Wondrous Woman? Wow!" She made a tiny squeak.

"Shhhhh." The older girl, for she was barely more than a girl herself, put a finger to her lips in the sign for quiet. "How are you tonight, Nancy?"

"I'm just great. But I don't have any cookies for you yet. Mom didn't make them this week."

"That's okay. Any time is fine."

For the next five minutes, Nancy prattled on about school and her daily trials. A seven-year-old with two older brothers had lots of things to complain about.

More serious matters emerged. Nancy revealed that she had told her mother about Wonderous Woman's late-night visits. So before too long, the visits had to stop. Time to zero in on the primary mission.

"How's your dad doing, Nancy?"

"Dad's all grouchy and crabby. Mom's worried about him and even cried once. She says Dad is married to his computer."

"That sounds serious. Is he only mad at mom, or everybody?"

"Everybody. Dad won't play, not even with Greg or Jimmy." Those were the brothers, who loomed large in Nancy's life.

Wondrous Woman asked a few more questions but couldn't figure out why Nancy's father was acting so oddly. Still, she did her best to encourage the little girl.

"Your parents will be fine."

They talked a bit longer, and then Wondrous Woman headed back to the window. "See you soon, Nancy. Take care."

The figure in the red-and-blue outfit climbed carefully down the drainpipe. She drew a black sweater out of a backpack stashed behind the broadleaf hedge at the foot of the driveway, shrugged into it and buttoned it up. Slinging the backpack over her shoulders, she jogged the eight blocks back to her CalSci house.

The elite Pasadena college called their dorms "houses." The residential units provided support and collaborative living in the high-pressure academic environment. Most CalSci students would privately agree that their informal house activities were the most engrossing part of campus life. Those stories were told and retold long after graduation.

One memorable band of conspirators in the sixties had disassembled a Volkswagen bug and reassembled it in a lab overnight. The frustrated college administration had to knock down part of a wall to get the car out of the building.

The young woman in the Wondrous Woman outfit carefully took off her costume and hung it in her closet, zipping her fanciest long-sleeved dress over it. No one would be touching that dress for months.

Her roommate, Janna, in the same sweats she wore to bed every night, was doing homework at her desk.

"Hey, Samantha. How'd it go?"

"No problems. Professor Rogers is being weird at home, just like in class. What the hell do you think is going on?"

"An affair? Wife troubles?"

Wondrous Woman offered another possibility. "His research? Maybe something's hitting the fan? Tonight the kid repeated that her mom says he's married to his computer." Dr. Rogers had a reputation for being an absent-minded professor, even on their campus, where distracted thinkers occasionally ran into walls or wore the same shirt for a week.

"Could be marital probs even if there's more. How's the house security?"

Wondrous Woman, now wearing a nightshirt, said, "Their security sucks. No motion detectors or lights, and the burglar alarm is only armed on the first floor."

Janna smiled. "Is there someplace I can hide near the house to check for WiFi leaks?"

"Sure."

The next night two CalSci students, equipped with backpacks, briskly walked the short distance into the neighborhood surrounding campus. Anyone seeing them would have assumed they were heading for an off-campus snack or study session.

It had been overcast with a light drizzle all day. At the Rogers' home, Nancy's window was almost completely shut.

After a whispered conversation the young women crouched behind the hedge and Janna produced a thin laptop from her backpack.

Samantha took out a black wraparound skirt from her own backpack and put it on. She kept a careful watch up and down the street.

For a while, nothing happened.

"Pssst! Dog walker," Samantha hissed.

Janna whipped the laptop into her backpack and the two women stood and began a slow stroll back toward campus.

"Evening," Janna said to the dog walker, barely visible in glowing streetlamps on the leafy street. The dog ignored them while the man mumbled something indistinguishable and the duo passed them by.

A couple of blocks away from campus, Samantha said "Did you have enough time? We could wait a half hour and go back."

"Nah. I got the basics. This needs The Goddess."

Everyone knows what a hacker looks like. They're skinny, kinda unhealthy, and studious, to put it mildly. They're also smart as hell and typically boys. Or men. But at CalSci, they're usually closer to boys.

The Goddess of Hacking—The Goddess for short—was tall with skin the color of mocha. She brandished a wild mass of kinky hair and a body any gym-lover would envy. Every male within a three-mile radius would tell you she was definitely female.

The next morning The Goddess, aka Alexis, was inhaling a cup of black coffee when her two housemates approached.

"You talking yet?" Samantha asked.

Normally The Goddess wasn't verbal until her second cup "Yumph."

Samantha took that as agreement and gave her the background. "First, I know I don't need to remind you, but I'm still helping you with PoliSci."

"Aw hell. Do I really wanna hear this?"

"You can say no. But we've been investigating. And you like Professor Rogers as much as the rest of us."

Samantha sketched in her adventures as Wondrous Woman.

Then she described the trip with Janna, junior-level hacker, to check out WiFi security at the Rogers home and what Professor Rogers was doing.

Janna picked up the story. "It's pitiful. His WiFi isn't even password-protected."

The Goddess put her coffee cup down and stared at them.

Janna continued. "Yes, believe it. I got in far enough to figure out WTF. He's gambling online."

"You're right," The Goddess said, taking another sip of coffee. "Pitiful and sad. He's a smart guy and he's nice. In-sane. How can the dude be so dumb?"

Samantha chipped in. "It's like, an addiction. You get started, it works out, and you can't stop. I have a cousin who was hooked on online poker. He got treatment or something, doesn't do it anymore. Goes to twelve-step groups and everything now."

The Goddess looked at the roommates. "So. We're gonna fix this. And here's the deal. I'll keep it confidential and—"

Samantha cut in. "Confidential about the gambling hack as well as Wondrous Woman. In return, you get PoliSci help for life. And Econ, if needed."

The Goddess stuck out her hand and Samantha shook it. Janna beamed.

Three days later, Rachel Rogers was loading dishes in the dishwasher and cleaning up the kitchen when her husband walked into the room, tears streaming down his face.

"Honey, what's the matter? What happened?"

"Come in the den, I have to tell you something."

Her husband walked her to his chair in front of the computer. Once she was seated, he tapped a key.

Bright colors filled the screen with elaborate graphics of a bull romping across the top. Rampaging Bull Casino obviously owned the site.

Below in black letters an inch high was the notice: Member

Balance 0.

Below that, in bright red letters two inches high the page screamed:

Membership Terminated.

This individual is no longer eligible for membership.

We are sorry for any inconvenience. Have a nice day.

"I owed this place six thousand dollars, honey."

"Oh, Tom." Rachel Rogers jumped up and wrapped her husband in a hug. He hugged her back just as fiercely.

"I kept trying to win it back. Of course, I never could. I owed even more than this to three other places. I couldn't see a way out."

His wife leaned back and looked him in the face. She hugged him again.

In a few minutes he pulled away gently. "Look at this."

Rogers sat in the chair himself and clicked through his favorite sites. All of them had the same notices: Balance 0, Ineligible for Membership.

"Look at these. I've never gone on any of these sites."

Gambling website after website popped up, with the notation: Individual Not Eligible for Future Membership.

Each one had a link next to it, for Gamblers Anonymous.

"Somebody ripped those first sites off for about thirty thousand dollars we don't have. Or paid them off. I have no idea."

Rachel Rogers squeezed her husband yet again. "Serves them right. They're preying on people who obviously have an addiction. And you do." She waited to see if her husband would protest.

Instead, he kissed her cheek. "I'll call Gamblers Anonymous tomorrow. I'm beat."

Two days later Janna and Wondrous Woman out of costume, aka Samantha, approached The Goddess with a tray. It held their breakfasts, a giant mug of black coffee, and the bagel they knew was The Goddess's favorite. Also on the tray was a small brown bag, clearly half full.

"You so totally did it. You are the best," Wondrous Woman said.

They raised their coffee mugs in a shared salute.

"You needed my skills, but you did a ton of the work before even bringing me in. You figured out Professor Rogers had to be rescued," The Goddess said modestly. "Did the prelim, and the second-story work."

Wondrous Woman smiled. "It was my pleasure."

The Goddess's face sobered. "There was more going on than we knew. His second favorite site was rigged to cheat. The stuff that's supposed to generate random numbers was programmed to pay off just enough to keep the suckers coming back. In other words, keep taking the money."

"No lie," Janna's eyes were wide.

"What'd you do?" asked Wondrous Woman.

"A little link from my research went right to the FBI. And that's not all."

"Tell," Janna said.

"He was suicidal. I found searches for painless ways to kill yourself."

Janna covered her mouth. "Oh, no."

There was a long pause.

Wondrous Woman broke the silence, reaching for the paper bag. "We saved a good man and a family. We punished the bad guys."

Her friends nodded.

Her face brightened. "Bonus. We've got goodies." She took plump oatmeal cookies out of the bag and handed one to each of her colleagues.

The Goddess took a bite. "These are amazing."

The trio took a moment to eat and consider their startling results.

Janna recovered first. "We are" she said, "Avenging Superheroes, right?" A big grin spread across her face.

Wondrous Woman shook her head. "No, no, can't be. Wondrous Woman's in the other universe. Not enough females in Avenging Supers, either."

The Goddess settled it. "Bunch of guys wrote it. Somebody'll buy out the other comic company, and it'll be one universe. We're just ahead of them."

They raised their coffee mugs again and toasted in unison, "Avenging Wondrous Women!"

THE BABY

Avril Adams

"Goodness, what a pretty baby. What an adorable baby," said Christine to Fiona, the baby's mother. "And hellooo, baby Scarlett," she said to the baby. "Aren't you a big, big girl?"

Christine thought Scarlett was a good name for the baby, with her unusually full head of red hair and her sky-blue eyes. Scarlett smelled wonderful, too, like baby powder dusted on warm sugar cookies. She tickled the baby's toes, reciting "This Little Piggy" with each tiny digit. When she touched the smallest toe and sang, "This little piggy cried wee, wee, wee, all the way home," the baby squealed with delight, her chubby legs pedaling the air. Scarlett burbled when Christine leaned over the crib rail and rubbed her face in the round, bare spot between the bitsy blue undershirt and the diaper.

Christine straightened, her huge grin fading when she looked at Fiona, who seemed exhausted with a weariness so deep it appeared ominous, like an encroaching illness. It was already one o'clock in the afternoon, and Fiona had answered the door of her apartment un-showered, wearing a dirty bathrobe, her hair an oily mess. There were dark circles under her eyes, and her skin had the pallor of boiled cod. Christine hardly recognized her old friend. She thought this new baby might be taking a lot out of her. Christine had been away in New York, earning a Ph.D. in zoology. She deeply regretted that she hadn't been there for the birth of Fiona's first baby, who had tragically died. She was glad she and her friend had reconnected since the birth of this second child.

"Let's get you some tea," said Christine. She urged Fiona into a chair in the living room and then marched into her friend's cluttered, claustrophobic kitchen. She set the kettle on to boil while she foraged in the fridge, drumming up stale bread and marmalade. Inside the fridge door were several bottles of Paxil and Xanax. Otherwise, there was only raw hamburger, old salad, condiments, and grapefruit juice. Instead of food, the fridge stored bottled formula and breast milk Fiona had pumped and saved for later. Christine remembered Fiona had complained that her nipples were raw from Scarlett's biting down so hard.

When the tea was ready, Christine brought it out on a tray with toast and jam. Fiona sat in an easy chair with her head against its floral chintz back, her eyes closed. She might have been asleep except that the downturned mouth suggested worry, not sleep.

"Make a space on your lap," said Christine. "I have something very nice for you."

Fiona looked at Christine with dull, submissive eyes. "You're such a good friend," she said.

Christine shushed her with a piece of toast, but just as Fiona tasted it, the baby began to cry. Scarlett howled lustily. Christine was impressed with its strength and urgency. "What a pair of lungs," she said. "She's either gonna be an opera singer, or a top sergeant." Fiona started to get up. Christine pressed her downward. "Eat," she said. "I'll take care of Scarlett."

Christine returned to the baby's room. When Scarlett's unfocused eyes swam in Christine's direction, she stopped crying. Christine picked her up and bounced her against her shoulder. Scarlett was heavier than she looked, by at least a couple of pounds. Christine rocked Scarlett for a while, humming a lullaby.

When Scarlett quieted, Christine lowered her into the crib.

The baby stuck a thumb in her mouth, but her other fist still thrashed defiantly, and Christine couldn't resist tucking her own pinkie under the fist's tiny fingers. The baby grasped it tightly and shook it as if it were a rattle. For a while, Christine cooed at Scarlett, but when she tried to remove her finger, the baby held on, even when Christine tugged. Christine was surprised the baby had such a robust grip. One by one, she had to peel the tiny fingers away.

When Christine returned to the living room, Fiona was asleep, truly and deeply asleep. Christine went to the room's small picture window. It was raining, and the dark clouds spoiled the view. She looked out over the rain-swollen Los Angeles River rushing below. On one side of the river a temporary holiday amusement park had been set up for the children of shoppers in the mall. Because of the downpour, the Ferris wheel and the bumper cars stood empty. In the distance, along the banks of the river, a line of blue bivouacs sheltered the homeless.

Christine watched the wildlife on the river for a while, then settled into an easy chair and picked up a book with a bright red cover, which was splayed open over its arm. It was about motherhood, written by a psychiatrist. The title of the opened chapter was "Sudden Infant Death, A Modern Perspective." Christine realized that Fiona had been reading it, hoping it might reveal something about why her friend's first baby had died.

She skimmed the chapters on medical issues and the importance of early mother-child bonding, but it was the next chapter that startled her. The title read "SIDS: Mishap or Murder?" The case study of a Mrs. X was explored. Christine had heard of SIDS but the possibility that a child's death could be anything but accidental had never occurred to her. Mrs. X had smothered three of her own children with no one any the wiser. It was only when she suffocated the infant of a neighbor who had hired her as a sitter that she was caught. Christine shivered as she read.

She realized that she hadn't been overly curious when the baby died, but she had offered advice to her friend that now seemed absurd and heartless: *Try to move on. You can have another.* Heavens, she thought, did she even recall the dead baby's name? Then, to her relief, she remembered it was Coral. Yes, Coral. Fiona had sent a card with a picture of the baby, red-headed and blue-eyed, shortly after she was born. Fiona had also sent a card when Coral died less than a year later. Christine was nearly finished with the chapter when Fiona awakened.

"I'm sorry," she said, "I fell asleep. What are you reading?"

"Oh, just...nothing, really." She put the book down. "Guess you needed some rest."

Just then, the baby began to cry. Whimpers quickly turned to wails.

"She's probably hungry," said Fiona, exhaustion creeping back into her voice. "Scarlett eats every hour now. She's awfully demanding."

Despite the short nap, Fiona seemed more haggard than before. The bags under her eyes had taken on a greenish tint. She shuffled into the kitchen, pulling her bathrobe tightly around her. Christine could hear her open the fridge, heard the tinkling of bottles being moved around. A pot was taken out of the cabinet and filled with water. The gas stove was turned on.

Christine went to check on Scarlett. The baby was sitting up in the crib, whimpering. She held one end of her pink rubber rattle and the other end was in her mouth. She was teething and drool dripped from the corners of her lips. When Christine approached the crib, the baby looked at her.

Christine picked her up and bounced her, noticing that her cotton shirt and her hair were soaked with sweat. With her free hand the baby smeared her sticky palm across Christine's nose and mouth. Christine felt the little girl's minuscule pink fingernails scratch along the skin below her eyes. The nails were too soft to hurt, but she didn't want one of them to catch inside her eyelids. With some effort she pulled the baby's hands away from her face.

Fiona appeared with the warmed bottle of breast milk. Her slippers were so silent over the carpet that Christine was taken by surprise. Fiona handed Christine the bottle.

"You do it, you feed her. She likes you."

Christine tested the milk on her arm before maneuvering the rubber nipple into Scarlett's mouth. The baby sucked once and began to cry again, her face scrunched into a knot of anguish. She squirmed, her tiny fists flailing against Christine's face.

Christine handed the bottle back to Fiona. She bounced Scarlett up and down, but this time the baby seemed inconsolable. "What's wrong with her?" said Christine. "She seemed fine a moment ago. I tested the milk on my arm. It was cool enough."

Fiona seemed to slump a little. "I don't know. She can get colicky. Sometimes she's sleepy. Maybe it's because it's *my* milk."

Christine stared at Fiona. "Don't be silly. You're overtired."

Christine walked around the room with Scarlett until the tension in the baby's body relaxed. Now Scarlett was struggling to stay awake. Christine took her back to her crib and covered her with the blanket. Soon she was fast asleep.

"I don't know how you do it," Christine said to Fiona as they returned to the living room. "I never knew the value of peace and quiet until now, in your apartment. Quiet is actually a thing, isn't it? Like negative space. So is peace. When they're there, you don't notice. It's when they're not there..."

Fiona interrupted. "Why don't you stay for a while?" She spoke quickly, persuasively. "We can have dinner, watch some television."

"Have dinner?" said Christine. "How? There's no food." She laughed. "Fiona, you *do* need somebody around. How about that Bernard fella, Scarlett's father?"

Fiona shook her head emphatically but said nothing.

Christine's voice expressed her exasperation. "Fiona, you shouldn't be here alone with the baby."

"We can order in?" blurted Fiona. "There's a Chinese place, The Red Dragon, around the corner on Glendale. We can order a Kung Pao something or other, with vegetables." She waved her hand, not caring.

"They wouldn't happen to have Mai Tais to go, would they?" Christine laughed.

They turned on the television and watched the news in silence, listening for the knock of the food delivery person. It arrived quickly and smelled good. Kung Pao chicken, beef with broccoli and steamed rice. Christine hadn't realized she was so hungry. They sat down again in front of the television with their food. Just then the baby began to bawl.

"Let her cry," Christine said. "A few tears never hurt anybody." But the bawling grew louder and louder and Christine thought Scarlett screamed with a fervor that was almost frightening. "I'll get it," she said. "I'll try the formula this time."

Christine went to the crib with the bottle of warm formula. When she held it out the baby reached for it and took it with both hands, poking it into her mouth. She sucked and burbled happily, keeping her eyes on Christine. Scarlett was quiet now. Christine thought she could bring her out while they ate and watched television.

When Christine appeared with the baby, Fiona reached for her, but the baby turned away and clung to Christine. When Fiona reached for the baby's chubby thighs, the baby kicked hard at her fingers with both feet.

Christine was perplexed but said, "I've got your little Hercules well in hand, Fiona, just relax." Christine didn't know why the infant son of Zeus popped into her mind at that moment or why she imagined the snakes Hera had sent to strangle him in his crib.

Christine held the baby on her lap and pushed the food around with chopsticks while Scarlett wriggled and reached for the cartons. Christine had only managed a few bites when she felt something warm and wet in her lap. She lifted Scarlett over her head.

"Diapers away." She blew on the baby's exposed belly. The baby giggled, and Christine swung her in the air again. The baby pumped her legs gleefully. Too late, she noticed Scarlett kick the food containers off the plates and onto the floor.

"Oh no," cried Fiona as the food sailed off the table. Tears welled over her lids, spilling trickles down her cheeks. "It's Scarlett," she sobbed. "She won't let me eat. She won't let me sleep. She blames me for Coral. She wants me dead." Fiona wept, barely able to catch her breath. Her outburst seemed to trigger the baby, who squalled and screamed in unison with her mother.

Christine sat Scarlett in the chair and scrambled to salvage something edible from the coffee table. All the chicken and beef and most of the rice had splattered onto the dirty carpet.

"It was my fault about the food, not Scarlett's," said Christine. "I was careless. I shouldn't have swung her around like that."

Christine knelt beside Fiona's chair, pulled her friend's head onto her shoulder. "Fiona," she said softly, "It's going to be all right. Think about what you're saying. How could she possibly want you dead?"

She settled Fiona into the chair. Scarlett had tipped sideways in the other chair, playing with the rattle.

Christine felt her emotions fraying. She was beginning to feel like a referee in a battle between opposing forces, which she knew was ridiculous. The bond between a mother and child was not dissoluble. Babies and mothers didn't struggle at cross purposes. The only will a baby might possess was the instinct for survival. The will of all sane mothers was the same. That was to protect the baby—the mother-child bond, right? But what if the baby wanted something else? What if the mother did, too? Christine felt confused. She wondered where Coral fit into the picture.

Christine instantly upbraided herself. Dissonant ideas weren't her forte. But she had to admit there was something odd, something impaired between these two that, like a software virus in a computer, had corrupted all of the DNA files. Maybe she could see it because she *wasn't* a mother, *wasn't* an insider, and didn't understand what was supposed to happen between a mother and her baby.

Christine turned off the news. She didn't want to hear about all the troubles in the world. When the TV was off, she realized the house was not only very quiet when both mother and baby were asleep, but the silence was somehow disquieting. The silence felt alive. She could hear the hard pellets of unseasonable hail scratching at the dirty window glass and the clock tinkling seven bells on the fake fireplace mantle.

Fiona stirred a bit, vulnerable the way she had been years ago when they were both no more than children.

"Fiona," Christine said. "Wake up, let's talk."

Her friend opened her eyes and stared glassily toward the ceiling.

"Fiona, we have to talk."

Fiona gave Christine a hooded look. "Christine, I'm so glad you're still here." She yawned and stretched. The dark circles under her eyes had only grown and darkened since the morning. "What do you want to talk about?"

Christine looked down at the paisley carpet, stained where the Chinese food had fallen, not knowing where to begin. "I...I...was reading your book earlier, the one you asked me about."

Fiona nodded, encouraging Christine to continue.

"I was reading the chapter on SIDS."

Fiona nodded again. "Uh-huh, Sudden Infant Death Syndrome."

"Fiona, I know I haven't been the best of friends to you—"

"Yes, you have."

"But I was wondering about your last...your first baby, Coral. How...I mean, why...did she die? I know I didn't ask a lot of questions about it at the time—I was terribly self-involved then. But I really want to know now."

Fiona fumbled with a tissue. "The doctor said it was SIDS. Babies just don't make it, sometimes. They just don't. But I knew there was nothing medically wrong with me. I knew I could have another...another Coral. You said that yourself, remember?"

"No, Fiona, that's not quite what I said. And babies don't 'not make it' for no reason."

Fiona's eyes searched the ceiling. "Coral had red hair. That's why I named her Coral. She had blue eyes, too, like Scarlett's. And they stayed that way—periwinkle—until she died. I don't know what color they would be now." She paused. Christine waited for her to finish. "The names of the shades of blue are beautiful, aren't they? Azure, cerulean…" Fiona was calm now, not agitated and overwrought the way she had been when the food had spilled. "Scarlett even wears Coral's clothes."

"I remember the picture of Coral you sent me," said Christine. "She did have beautiful blue eyes. And that red hair, like Scarlett's. She really is—was—so much like Scarlett. What happened to her?"

"I don't know." Fiona picked at the stitching on her chair with bitten nails. "I gave her a bath as I always did, and then I put her to bed. I laid her down on her tummy and went into the kitchen to do the dishes."

"When did you realize something was wrong?"

"I…I…the next morning. I was so busy. There was so much to do."

Christine wondered why Fiona had waited all night to check on Coral. "When did you call the police?"

"I didn't. She was so cold and she wouldn't wake up so I took her to the emergency room. They said she was already dead. *They* called the police."

"Did you do something to Coral?"

Fiona took a moment to answer and when she did Christine felt the icy blade of her penetrating stare.

"No."

"Was it an accident?"

"Of course," Fiona snapped. "The doctors said she just stopped breathing. But Scarlett doesn't believe it was an accident. She wants me to die for it."

Christine sighed. She wondered if guilt over Coral was driving Fiona's crazy ideas. "I saw your medication in the kitchen. Are you taking it?"

"I am," Fiona said. "I take it all the time. I just did."

Not really listening to Fiona now, alarms going off like fire bells in her head, Christine said, "I'll get it for you." She walked back into the cramped kitchen, thought about making more toast and tea, thought about calling someone, anyone. But who? She didn't want to leave Fiona alone with the baby. If Fiona was somehow disturbed, the baby was in danger.

She picked up Fiona's medication and went back into the living room. She read out loud from the label, "Take one every four hours, as needed," and held the bottle out to Fiona. The bottle looked half full. Christine thought she had taken some.

Fiona pushed away the bottle.

Christine wanted to put Scarlett on the floor. She was strong enough to crawl and pull herself up, but the carpet was so soiled Christine had second thoughts. She pulled Scarlett out of the chair and pressed her against her chest. The baby was as warm as a biscuit inside her jumper and damp with salt-glazed sweat.

Scarlett pulled at Christine's long dark locks until Christine's face was buried in the baby's shoulder. Scarlett burbled happily as she reached for Christine's ears, clapping her hands when she found them. She gripped Christine's collar, and her eyes swam across Christine's face until they settled on her eyes and held.

Christine saw something in the baby's eyes, a subtle shift of acumen, a colluding spirit. She had never noticed that before. Was it true of *all* babies or just *this* one?

Christine recognized that she and Scarlett were fellow creatures of an uncharted species of sensitive souls who had a deep under- standing of each other. As much as she cared for Fiona, Christine now realized some stroke of luck or fate had brought her here. She belonged to the baby, and the baby belonged to her.

Christine put Scarlett down on the hardwood part of the floor that surrounded the carpet. She watched her crawl for a moment, scuttling on all fours, working her way around the chair legs. Scarlett found a shoe under the sofa, pulled it out and banged it hard against the floor. She crawled away and pulled herself up on the leg of the coffee table, turning in triumph to look at the women.

Fiona said, "She knows all about you. She knows who you are."

Christine was guarded. "What? Knows who I am? What does that even mean?"

"She's an old soul. She knows who everyone is," said Fiona.

"Don't be silly. She's a baby, she likes anyone who plays with her."

"Maybe," said Fiona. "But it's more than that." She yawned. "It's been so ugly out, I haven't been out for the mail in days. You wouldn't mind, would you, watching Scarlett while I run out for the mail? I'm expecting a check and I could use the air."

"Not at all," said Christine, distractedly. She was still disturbed by what she had come to believe about Scarlett.

Fiona got up for the first time in hours, retrieving her coat and an umbrella. She opened the apartment door and turned to say, "I'll be right back."

Christine watched Scarlett also hasten toward the door. She scuttered forward in such a way that if you weren't paying attention, you wouldn't notice how quickly she moved. Christine heard the crack of thunder and saw the flash of lightning. She turned away for just a moment to witness nature's ferocious display, thinking whatever Scarlett intended, it would be what it would be, and Christine would be there to pick up the pieces. Then she heard the soft thump of a body falling, over and over, and Fiona's scream as she tumbled headlong down the stairs.

THE UNKINDEST CUT

L.H. Dillman

June 30

Dear Peter,

Today marks two years since I last saw you—the longest twenty-four months I've ever had to endure. Today also marks two weeks since I moved. I suspect you are not as unhappy where you are as I am in my new home.

I start each day with an affirmation and positive thinking, but the reality of my situation soon sets in. By afternoon I either have the indigo blues or am crimson with anger. Dinner helps level my mood. Then my old nemesis, insomnia, sets me up for another wild day. I could seek pharmaceutical relief, but I won't. No zombiedom for me, thank you.

Sorry to begin on such a gloomy note, my love. Melancholy is not something with which you've ever had to wrestle, is it?

This morning, to lift my spirits and to burn off excess calories (carbohydrates abound!), I attempted a hip-hop exercise class led by one of the other "guests." I lasted twenty minutes. It turns out that, in addition to carrying a few extra pounds, I have lousy rhythm. Predictable for a fifty-four-year-old white woman, I suppose. I stood out like a damp turd on a damask tablecloth.

Or, more fittingly, like a damask tablecloth on a damp turd.

I simply don't fit in at Chick-ie-Woe, the local sobriquet for the Chino Correctional Institute for Women and the cleverest utterance I've heard since I got here. The prison lies a mere sixty-five miles east of Los Angeles, but it might as well be on Mars. The British accent that has served me so well since I landed in America—and which no doubt played a part in your decision to hire me at Palisades Prep—is now a liability. I am mocked and taunted daily. One young lady (using the term loosely) will cross the yard to describe what she'd like to do to my "Enormous English Arse" in a Cockney accent by way of Hoboken. Another bright bulb, whom I cannot avoid because she works in the cafeteria, inquires loudly after Victoria Beckham or Sir Paul, then brays like a donkey in coveralls. Yesterday, I was offered a "spot of tea"—urine in a paper cup.

I've really no one to talk to. My cell mate, a forty-year-old former drug dealer who goes by "Bee," graces me with a syllable or two per day. I fear I'll soon go off my trolley.

Oh, what I wouldn't give for one more evening with you, Peter. I picture a dinner at Ivy by the Shore—flutes of champagne upon arrival, waiters in pink oxford shirts and floral-print neckties, tables laid with crisp linen and sterling flatware. I see us sharing a ribeye served rare while dissecting the new Tarantino film. Over dessert, you seek my advice on the latest scandal at Prep—which does *not* involve your banging a teacher. Then I pick up the *exorbitant* check, which I can do, as I've gone on to teach English at an even more posh academy. Afterward, we stroll along Ocean Avenue, stop below a palm tree for a kiss...

Ah, perchance to dream...

If you were to visit Chick-ie-Woe at dinnertime, you'd find me pushing a plastic tray along aluminum rails, pausing for a slice of green-tinged turkey and a slop of reconstituted potatoes, then scurrying to find a seat where I might eat unmolested. I use "molested" in the sense of nagging and bullying, not sex—though there is plenty of that going on, judging by the nightly moans and groans. Good God, the all-girls boarding school in Essex was positively celibate by comparison.

Apropos of sounds, the last bell has just rung. Five minutes to lights out.

I shall say good night and post this letter in the a.m.

With love always,

Your English Rose,

Maggie

July 6

Dear Peter,

A quick note to share some good news:

My lawyer called to say he's just filed the appellate brief and is even more optimistic now than when he took the case. David Rothman, Esq., thinks it likely that my conviction will be tossed, and, if the court of appeal agrees with him about the evidence being illegally seized, the prosecutors may choose not to refile the charges because they cannot win without the tainted evidence. Nor should they. A woman's home is her castle, don't you agree? This is not the way it works in Great Britain, unfortunately.

In other words, Peter, I might soon be a free woman! Mind you, "soon" could be several months. You would caution me not to count my chickens, and of course you'd be right. Still, it's lovely to have reason to hope. Without hope, there is nothing. That way madness lies.

Yours forever,

Maggie

July 14

Happy Bastille Day, *Mon Cher!*

I imagine you lounging in the sunshine, sipping Bordeaux, the scent of lavender on the breeze. Here at Chick-ie-Woe, I make do with the aroma of bleach and a swig of cranberry juice—always on tap due to its properties as a deterrent to urinary tract infections (not mine, of course).

Do you ever think about our week in France? I'd been teaching at Prep for less than a semester when you asked me to be the third chaperone for the senior class trip to Paris. You must've noticed that I was already smitten. You couldn't have been fooled by the coincidental encounters in the car park, the serendipitous meetings in the lunchroom, my too-eager smiles and too-clever *bon mots*. I acted like a gobshite schoolgirl!

I was "low-hanging fruit," as you Americans say. And you were right there to pick me.

Off we jetted, the two of us plus another teacher and thirty of the most entitled adolescents on God's Green Earth. For two days, my signals went unheeded, radio waves broadcast to deep space. I feared I'd misread you. Then, on day three, whilst standing in a crowded gallery at the Louvre, I felt you cup my bum with both hands. Instead of leaping aside, I pushed backward, inviting your fingers to find their way. And they did. It was all I could manage not to melt to my knees. The memory still serves a purpose.

That night at the hotel, we went at it like randy rabbits. And the next night and the next. I recall your assuring me, when I fretted about being discovered by the students, that their rooms were at the far end of the hall. I wondered if you'd arranged that, and I figured I wasn't the first new hire to fall for the debonair and single Head of School—or to shag him whilst on a school junket. When I hinted at the topic, you assured me that my intellect and personality set me apart from any predecessors. All the attention made me feel twenty years younger. I remember wishing we could stay.

But duty called.

On our first day back, as we were dressing for work, you surprised me with a new set of rules: we couldn't be seen going home together or even leaving campus at the same time.

I froze, knickers about my knees. "Today, you mean?"

"From here on out. And best not to call my office or text me during the day. Unless it's an emergency. No one can know we're involved."

"Seems rather harsh."

"It's school policy." You came over to kiss my neck. "Well, not in so many words. I think it says, 'Intimate relations with subordinates are discouraged.'"

"Discouraged is not the same as prohibited."

"I know," you said, lips moving down my chest. "But I don't want to ruffle any feathers on the Board, not with my contract coming up for renewal. I'm sorry, Maggie."

"When will I see you then?"

"Weekends and hopefully a couple of nights during the week," you said, biting my nipple.

I wanted more of you, and I didn't like the subterfuge, but I went along. And, despite all the restrictions, I was happy. I know in my heart you were, as well. We were greater than the sum of our parts, Peter. We had something rare, something worth keeping.

I wonder where we would be now if a certain Mademoiselle Stacie Fenton had not applied to teach Phys. Ed. at Palisades Prep, or if you hadn't hired her, or if her essential nature weren't so base, or if you'd kept your trousers zipped.

I will let you mull that over.

Yours truly,

Margaret

P.S. Stacie? Seriously? The spelling alone should have warned you off. That which we call a scrubber by any other name would smell as foul.

July 21

Dear Peter,

I hope you don't mind hearing from me so often. I've been feeling proper narky and writing letters longhand is supposed to help. Bee let me know this morning that she's applied for a cell change. I'd thought we were finally developing something of a friendship. Last week she made me a lanyard with my initials embedded—I'll show it to you someday. I asked why she wanted to move, and she said she hopes to be paired with an incoming inmate, a young woman named "Coco" whose arrival has the entire block excited. Evidently, Coco is not only a convicted fraudster but an "Instagram Star" with a social media empire. (Who could have predicted such a thing? Aldous Huxley meets Rupert Murdoch with a dollop of Kim Kardashian. Heaven help us.)

"She's like a digital-age Martha Stewart, then," I suggested to Bee.

"Who?"

And there you have it.

Altogether too depressing. Perhaps a walk 'round the yard will help.

Signing off with affection,
Your Margaret

July 27

Dear Peter,

Today I met someone who reminded me of you—or, rather, of how I picture you twenty years ago. He's a state psychiatrist: Dr. Daniel Cohen. Deep-set brown eyes, a wide mouth, and a close-cropped beard—handsome, reasonably intelligent, and superficially charming. I'd been told only that Dr. Cohen meets with each new inmate within thirty days of her arrival.

"Welcome to Chino, Ms. Thorne," Cohen said from the opposite chair. We were in a dingy little conference room in the main building. The air smelled stale, and the overhead lightbox flickered like an anemic strobe.

"Thank you," I said, shielding my eyes.

"How do you like it here so far?"

"I would have preferred the port side and a balcony."

Puzzlement. Then a chuckle. "Good one." He glanced at his clipboard. "Are you working on your Personal Progress Plan?"

"Why? So that someday I'll be deemed ready to rejoin society?"

"That's one reason."

"Come now, doctor. You've read my file. I won't be leaving here on two feet unless my conviction is tossed out, and believe me, if that happens, I won't be filling out any of your damned forms."

"Every inmate needs a Progress Plan, irregardless of the length—"

"Irrespective."

"Irrespective. Right. Very sharp." Cohen cleared his throat. "There's no need for hostility, Ms. Thorne. I'm just trying to get to know you."

Out in the hall, a crash, profanity, a thud. I swung around to look at the door, but Cohen didn't even glance in that direction. One becomes inured.

"Have you ever been under the care of a psychiatrist?" he asked.

"Absolutely not. I'm entirely sane." It dawned on me that Cohen might be there to assess whether I belong in one of those asylums for homicidal maniacs. I should find out if the state can reassign me even though I specifically chose *not* to plead not guilty by reason of insanity.

"I'm not talking about legal insanity," he said. "Only about managing any ongoing mental health issues—"

"Did someone lodge a complaint against me?"

"Is there a reason they might have?"

"People fear that which they don't understand."

"Are you hard to understand, Ms. Thorne?" The condescension was unmistakable.

"People often underestimate me, usually to their detriment."

He regarded me for a long moment, then referred to his clipboard. "How do you feel about Peter McMillan?"

"I will not discuss him." *You are off limits to shrinks, Peter.*

"All right. How do you feel about Stacie Fenton?"

The instant her name left his lips, the little chippy materialized before me—tan, long legs, big smile, blond hair in a ponytail. A hideous hallucination, a bimbo hologram. I blinked her away and said, "I've no feelings about her one way or t'other."

Then I followed Cohen's gaze to my fingers, to the crescent cuts my nails were carving in the faux-leather arms of my chair. "I'm not especially fond of her," I admitted.

"Why's that?"

Stacie Fenton had ruined my life. *Did Cohen not know this?* "She had the bad manners to insult me in public."

"Where was this?"

"At the gala—Palisade Prep's annual fundraiser. Big hotel ballroom with an orchestra, hundreds of parents in attendance."

"Was she a parent?"

"Miss Fenton was on the faculty, if you want to call a gymnastics coach 'faculty,'" I said, rubbing my pounding temples. My head ached from the flickering fluorescent bulb. "She wasn't taken at all seriously—until then."

"What happened?"

"She paraded around on his arm as if she were Elizabeth the Second." *Uneasy lies the head that wears the crown.*

"Peter McMillan's arm?"

"It was a violation of school policy!"

"Dating the headmaster?"

"If the rule was going to be broken, it should have been by me. I was humiliated!"

"Do you think she did it to hurt you?"

"I expect she didn't give a whit for anyone's welfare but her own. Maybe she wanted the status. Maybe she wanted a father figure. I don't know. That's your department, doctor."

"Peter McMillan bore some responsibility, didn't he?"

I turned away.

"Ms. Thorne? What about Peter?"

I glowered at the wall.

"Hell hath no fury, eh?"

I spun back around, and I swear, Peter, I thought it was you sitting there. Another optical illusion. Cohen lurched backward with a yelp, whereupon a C.O. stormed in, hand on her taser.

"So sorry," I said. "Lost my balance. The lights have me all wobbly. Didn't mean to alarm anyone."

Cohen left the room pale as a parsnip.

"See you next time, doc," I called cheerfully, as the C.O. slapped on the restraints.

They think they've got me figured out, Peter, but they haven't.

Yours always,
Margaret.

October 20

Dear Peter,

The reason I haven't written in such a long time is that I spent the last sixty days in "Administrative Isolation," also known as "Solitary Confinement" or "The Hole." This explains the lapse on my end; what's your excuse? Ho. Ho. The good news is that I'm down to one hundred thirty-three pounds. Practically a mannequin. Ready to coach gymnastics!

I oughtn't make light of the experience, even in jest, as I expect the C.O.s will be reading my mail. My punishment was cruel and *completely unjustified* because I acted in self-defense. Also, the situation was entirely within management's power to prevent. All they had to do was provide secure shower stalls and/or assign competent C.O.s to oversee the loo.

But *no*.

Coco cornered me in the shower. I knew what she wanted because she'd tried it before, and I'd managed to get away. This time we were alone, and I was totally starkers. I slapped and shoved, but she was strong and persistent. Luckily, the faucet handle was loose. The spokes fit snugly between my knuckles. Every blow was necessary, Peter, every last one.

I am considering a lawsuit against management. Do you see that, C.O.?

They let me out at seven this morning. I'd barely set foot in my cell when Warden Sanford summoned me to a meeting. (Terry Sanford is a big bull herself, if you want my opinion.) Her office is in the main wing and rather underwhelming. Indoor-outdoor carpeting, cheap furniture, the requisite flags, official-looking photographs of her with various individuals whom I assumed to be politicians and bureaucrats.

"Have a seat," Sanford said, appraising me through thick spectacles. "And take a look at these." She slid a couple of color prints across the desk. They were photos taken at the scene. It's true the shower looked like an abattoir, but any ninth grader knows that the face bleeds profusely due to the abundance of capillaries.

"Coco might not have any sight in her left eye," Sanford said. "What do you have to say to that?"

"She started it."

"You totally overreacted. You went crazy on her, Thorne. Almost as extreme as the crime that landed you here."

I knew better than to respond.

"Why am I not hearing remorse?" Sanford asked. "You had

sixty days to reflect on it. You could at least *pretend* you're sorry."

"Actually," I said, sitting up tall, "I'm more determined than ever not to tolerate assaults and indignities."

She jabbed her finger in my direction. "You've got a mouth on you. I oughtta send you back to The Hole."

I started to warn her about petty punishments when the phone on her desk buzzed three times. She waved me to silence and picked up. "Yes?" She turned her distasteful gaze to me. "Well, put him on." As she listened, her face drained of color. "Uh-huh...When?...No kidding...Okay, yeah. Thanks." She hung up, clearly gobsmacked.

"What?"

"Your appeal, it's been granted. Judgment of conviction reversed by a vote of two to one."

My heart did a catapult. "Really?"

"I find it hard to believe, too, but the corrections office got an email and a fax from your attorney last night."

"Am I free to go, then?"

"Not hardly," she said with a snort. "Considering the brutality of your offense, I gotta believe the D.A.'s office will refile a one-eighty-seven. You're gonna breathe your last breath here, Thorne."

I smirked, remembering what Rothman had told me: if the court of appeal rules the police illegally seized the dangly bits (your wee little willy and pathetic old prunes), the D.A. cannot win a retrial.

"How long until they decide?" I asked.

"Thirty days, maximum. By law."

One more month, Peter. Sadly, I won't be seeing you in person when I get out. I'd like to have that little chat, but it shall have to be at the cemetery.

Until then,

Yours,

Margaret

October 30

Dear Peter,

I'm being released tomorrow! Free as a bird. No retrial. It's time for celebration—for me; not so much for Stacie Fenton. I shall find her, wherever she may be. What then, you may ask. As old Lear put it: I shall do such things, yet I know not, but they shall be the terrors of the earth.

    M.

FUNERAL GAMES

Hal Bodner

"I cannot believe that necrophiliac trollop did it again."

Simon, my funeral director, wisely kept his eyes on the screen hanging on the office wall. It usually featured a tastefully produced sales video on a constant loop, something to subtly prompt the family to add options without our having to mention them. This morning, it was tuned to the local news instead, and my blood pressure was rising by leaps and bounds.

"Julia Shrike?" he asked.

"How many necrophiliac trollops do you know?"

"Necrophilia? Isn't that a little over-the-top, Mickey? Even for you?"

"Do you know what she did?" I raged.

"She stole the Arthur Campion funeral." Simon said it as if by rote.

"And the Priscilla Markham service," I reminded him.

"And Priscilla Markham," he sighed.

"And what about...?"

"I know, Mickey. I know. Harrison Harkness. Garret Garland and his mistress."

I closed my eyes and breathed in deeply, wistfully.

"Do you know how gorgeous that service would have been? Side-by-side graves, each crowned by a marble figure reaching longingly for the other. Their fingertips never quite touching. So exquisitely romantic. So lusciously lucrative."

I savored the mental image for a moment before continuing, somewhat sourly. "Suicide pacts were a whole new market, just itching to be exploited before that harridan screwed things up."

"I know," Simon said, tiredly. "Just like the pizza ads. Two for the price of one. You've told me a dozen times."

"Julia Shrike destroyed that dream."

"Please, Mickey. Don't start in again."

"She hijacked a hearse! Who *does that*?"

"You need to calm down."

"Do I? Do you know what I had to go through to close the Kyle Bee pre-need contract? God it was beautiful! They went for everything. Embalming, plus the deluxe cosmetics package. The Empire Cherry Wood casket with the ecru velvet lining *and* the sterling silver electroplated fittings. Top-of-the-line floral arrangements for the service. A plot in one of our best locations. Then the damned fool overdoses, and practically before the EMTs can yank his head out of the toilet...*look what she did!*"

Speechless with rage, I pointed at the screen.

Kyle Bee's funeral had turned out to be a bigger Industry event than the last three Oscars put together. Twenty-five hundred Hollywood types had stuffed themselves into the church for the funeral, all of them desperate to see and be seen. Outside Hollywood Memorial Gardens, another four thousand of Kyle's fans clamored to pay their respects, kept at bay by private security guards specially hired for the occasion and undoubtedly billed to the estate at a healthy profit. For the past two hours, a mile-and-a-half-long funeral procession had been making its way toward the cemetery with such sedate and lugubrious pomp that the traffic trying to cross Wilshire Boulevard at La Cienega was backed up halfway to LAX.

The She-Bees, the sexually frustrated, mostly teenaged members of Kyle's fan club, were out in force. Clad in their distinctive costumes, they engaged in a bizarre competition to prove who could show the most outrageously dramatic display of grief for their fallen idol. After a tower of bouquets, teddy bears, and women's underwear collapsed under its own weight and buried them alive, I felt that a compelling case could be made to declare the deceased pair of USC sorority sisters the unofficial winners.

Worse, in every photo of the event, in every shot of the milling crowd, and in every second of footage of the two girls meeting their doom under the mound of stuffed animals and daisies, the words *Hollywood Gardens Memorial Park* could clearly be seen in the background, emblazoned above the cemetery gates in four-foot-high letters.

You can't buy publicity like that. Lord knows, I've tried.

And Julia-Fucking-Shrike was getting it for free.

"He was so young," I said, dolefully. "And you *know* how their popularity goes through the roof when they die before thirty! Look at James Dean. Only three pictures and the man is a veritable god. If *only* we could get *him*!"

"Forget it, Mickey. He's in Indiana. With his family."

"Indiana? What good does that do us?" I fumed and shook my finger at the screen. "Are you watching this, Simon? Every one of those fans is a potential client. Lost. *That* is what profit looks like when it's going to *someone else*!"

"Maybe we could offer a discount to the families of the two fan-girls in the bumble bee costumes? It might bring us some publicity..."

"Oh, that's just brilliant," I said with a withering glare. "We can put signed photos of Kyle Bee into their hands just before we cremate them, and bury them in little beehive shaped caskets..." I allowed my frustration to get the better of me, "even though *he* is at *Hollywood Fucking Gardens!*"

I fumed for a few minutes longer before I realized that I had to take action.

"Where are you going?" Simon asked as I stormed toward the door.

"Howard Horowitz."

"Uh, is that a good idea? I mean, with the mood you're in?"

"I've got to do something. If Julia steals any more business from us, you and I will have new careers starving at the corner of Santa Monica and Vine, praying for a washed-up sitcom star to trade us Happy Meals for blow-jobs. Wish me luck."

"Good luck."

"Hah!" I shot back as I stormed toward my car. "The only luck I need is for Julia Shrike to trip and fall into one of her own graves."

Southern California's funeral industry is viciously competitive when it comes to celebrity funerals. People measure a memorial park's cachet by how many stars are buried on-site. Needless to say, the plots and crypts are priced accordingly. It never fails to astonish me how many people will pay top dollar to spend their eternal rest within spitting distance of a rock star when, in life, they'd have been outraged by the loud parties next door and called the police on the groupies throwing up on their lawn.

Ironically, I started out in the business at Hollywood Gardens—which was currently where Julia Shrike made her lair. We actually worked together for a while, and in the beginning, at least, I think we might even have liked each other. She was just past her twentieth birthday, a tiny little thing whose head barely reached the level of my chest. But she was absolutely gorgeous, and she exuded a sensual aura that was both tempting and frightening. For an eighteen-year-old boy without much experience, Julia was a lot like autoerotic asphyxiation. You know it's dangerous, but you can't help wondering.

Once she decided she wanted me, I didn't stand a chance.

Our affair was as brief as it was intense, lasting a scant twelve hours or so. The next morning, I'd barely finished getting untangled from her Egyptian cotton sheets when she booted me out of her apartment with nothing but a copy of the *L.A. Weekly* to cover my privates.

I never understood what I'd done to earn her enmity. I mean, even as close to virginal as I was, I couldn't have been *that* bad in bed! Nevertheless, she embarked on a campaign against me at work, hounding me for incompetence, accusing me of theft, and implying that I'd had inappropriate relations with clients. Since her uncle and aunt owned the place, I couldn't very well expect them to come to my rescue so, when the harassment became too much, I quit and took a job at a different cemetery.

In the intervening years, Julia had used tactics that would curdle the embalming fluid in a corpse's veins to seize control of Hollywood Gardens, and I had mortgaged myself to the hilt to buy Sunset Rest. As soon as Julia found out I was the new owner, she revived her campaign to ruin me. For the past eighteen months, my loathing of her had steadily grown to match her hatred of me.

I intercepted Howard Horowitz in the hallway outside his office, just as he was returning from lunch. When he saw me, he tried to sneak back into the elevator, but I was too quick for him.

"Howard! How are your kids enjoying those annual passes to Harry Potter World?"

"Uh...They love 'em, Mickey. What are you doing here?"

When someone famous dies, their business managers often have more influence than the families when it comes to deciding where they'll rest for eternity. Howard, however, was an anomaly in show business; he couldn't be bribed, at least not outright. To keep Sunset Rest Memorial Park near the top of his referral list, I never missed his kids' birthdays or failed to send them pricey Christmas presents. As they got older, the things they wanted got more expensive. God help me, once they were old enough to drive.

"I think you know, Howard."

"Look, Mickey..." He took me by the elbow and hustled me down the hall and into what I first thought was an unused office.

"A supply closet? Seriously, Howard? I'm not accustomed to taking meetings in rooms with buckets."

"I don't want you to make a scene."

"A scene? Me?" I asked, the picture of innocence.

"You know how you get, Mickey."

"How do I get, Howard? Upset? Hurt? Betrayed?"

"Look," he said, resigned, "I know you're here about Kyle Bee..."

"Kyle Bee...Kyle Bee." I pretended to search my memory. "Hmm, I seem to remember that Sunset Rest had a pre-need arrangement with someone named Bee."

"Please, don't be like that, Mickey. He bought burial insurance. I checked. I'd never want you to lose a buck on my account. They'll pay off your contract in full."

"That's not the point! We *need* him at Sunset Rest."

He shook his head. "Ain't gonna happen. Hey!" He brightened. "I'll tell you what. Lana Larkin just kicked it. One of the other old biddies at the Old Actors' Home was worried that Larkin didn't finish her dessert and spooned tapioca pudding into her respirator."

I made a rude noise and rolled my eyes. "Oh, please!. Larkin was a second-rate actress on a forty-year-old TV series. Anyone who'd pay to be near her is already long dead. Kyle Bee though. Do you know how many plots I could have sold? At least—"

He cut me off before I could work up more steam.

"I tried, Mickey. Once Julia got her claws into them, there was nothing I could do."

"How did she do it? Threats? Blackmail? Holding the family pets hostage?"

"I don't know," he said miserably. "He wasn't quite dead when they pulled him out of the john, so they had him on life support for two weeks. I guess that gave her enough time to work on the family."

"You're avoiding the question."

He shrugged uncomfortably. "Now, don't go giving yourself a stroke, Mickey. It's probably only a rumor."

I folded my arms across my chest and glared.

"She got them all riled up about something to do with your

endowment fund."

"*My* endowment?"

He nodded, miserably. "Embezzlement. Now wait! Before you fly off the handle...from what I hear, she didn't actually accuse you of anything. She just created enough doubt so that Bee's family was worried about the negative publicity if Sunset Rest got investigated."

My jaw dropped. Even for Julia, that was low.

"Believe me, I did my best. Please, Mickey, take Larkin as a gift. I know it's not much, but..."

"Fine, I said, and added a begrudging, "Thanks."

"The next one, Mickey. I promise," he called after me as I stalked toward the elevator.

Stealing clients and diverting funeral processions was one thing. Calling my integrity into question was another. Unfortunately, Julia had a lot more money than I did, and her PR machine was brutal. If I even thought about suing her, she'd bury me in a shroud of negative publicity. Even if I won, I'd lose.

One thing was certain though, I couldn't tolerate Julia Shrike's interference any longer. I had to do something about it. The question was...what?

Two weeks later, I heard from a wannabe starlet whose day job was at the County Coroner's Office. For the past few years, I'd been footing the bill for her acting classes in exchange for the occasional tip. When I'd recently complained that the monthly checks were starting to approach the annual tuition of Harvard or Yale, she promised to find a way to give me a return on my investment.

The bolt of lightning that hit the generator on the set of the remake of *The Towering Inferno* was just the thing to do it. The explosion French-fried a half dozen members of the crew and several of the actors, including Pookie Pruitt, star of the Emmy Award-winning television show, *Pookie's Place*, who was making his first foray onto the big screen. I was so pleased to get her call that I promised to pony up for a few extra voice lessons just to show my appreciation.

That night, I conscripted Simon into accompanying me on a clandestine visit to Hollywood Gardens.

"This is insane, Mickey," Simon complained.

"No. It's not insane. It's revenge."

"It's disrespectful, is what it is."

"Shut up and keep going. We need to finish before sunrise."

"I should have known it."

Simon's griping was developing a distinct whine. I tolerated it because he was doing most of the digging.

"When you didn't say a word about Julia swooping in to grab Pruitt and the other actors, I should have known you had something crazy up your sleeve."

"Crazy? I think not!" I crowed. "It's brilliant!"

I adjusted the lantern again to make sure most of the light was directed into the grave.

"Will you quit it," Simon continued to grouse. "You're blinding me with that thing."

"Bitch, bitch, bitch. First you can't see where you're digging. Now there's too much light. Make up your mind."

"Oh, I have," Simon said, in tandem with the thump of the shovel on the coffin lid. "I've decided that this is where you take over."

"Me?" I was aghast. "You can't possibly expect me to climb in there. I'm wearing six-hundred-dollar loafers!"

"You should have thought about that before we started." Simon clambered out of the grave. "So far, if we get caught, all they've got me for is trespass and maybe criminal mischief. It'll ruin my career faster than you can say Jessica Mitford, but at least I won't go to jail."

"No one is going to jail."

"That's right," he nodded. "Look, I'll even help you haul the casket out of the hole, but that's as far as I go. If I put one finger on that corpse, it's officially grave robbing or, worse, desecration. Fifty grand and five years in prison. This was your idea, Mickey.

You can risk your own ass."

"I think you just made up all that legal stuff because you're getting cold feet," I said pettishly. "Besides, I have no intention of desecrating anything."

Carefully, so as not to scuff my Cole Haans, I climbed down into the grave, and winced when, speaking of cold feet, my right foot sank up to the ankle in mud.

"I'm just going to...scatter a few bits here and there. See? No desecration. Just scattering. I don't even think scattering is a real crime. Pass me a casket key."

"That's not a good idea, Mickey. Your average grave robber isn't going to be walking around with a casket key in his pocket."

"We're not trying to pin it on some random ghoul, you ninny. We're trying to make it look like Julia cut corners and buried him too close to the surface."

"Without a casket?"

"Exactly! Obviously, they won't be able to prove anything against her. We're just going to create the impression that Julia dumped Pookie Pruitt's body in the dirt so she could resell the coffin. In the meantime, we'll take the casket back to our place and chuck it into the crematorium. No one will ever know it was us."

"I'm not so sure, Mickey. A lot of people were at the funeral. They saw the open grave. Does it make sense that she'd go to the trouble of re-opening it just to get at the coffin?"

"It doesn't have to make sense," I snapped. "It just has to start people wondering. Create doubt. Besides, who says she had to reopen the grave? No one ever sticks around for it to be filled in. Who's to say she didn't wait until after the last mourner was gone, evict the corpse, and put the coffin back into her showroom? A few swipes with some Lemon Pledge, a spritz or two of Fabreeze, and you're good to go."

He tossed me the hex key and I inserted it into the coffin lock.

"I can see it now," I gloated. "Tomorrow morning, sometime during the funerals for Pookie's fellow cast members, some lucky fan is going to stumble over a recognizable piece of poor Pookie's corpse and all hell is going to break loose. Remember that mess out at Mountainview Cemetery a few years ago? When the bodies started popping out of the ground? The place was ruined!"

I allowed myself a satisfied snicker as I struggled with the coffin lid.

"You should count yourself lucky, Mickey," Simon sighed. "If the burials tomorrow weren't practically on top of Pookie's grave, it wouldn't have worked."

"It hasn't worked yet," I cautioned him.

The angle was bad, and there wasn't much room between the sides of the casket and the dirt walls, but at the sacrifice of my other loafer, I was able to get the lid open.

"Not a half bad job," I had to admit when I got my first look at the corpse. "Though if he'd been at Sunset Rest, I'd have talked them out of burying him in the costume and make-up."

"What is he supposed to be?" Simon peered over the edge of the grave. "A squirrel?"

"Chipmunk," I said. "*Pookie's Place* is a kids' show. Hand me the hacksaw and the pliers, will you?"

Long before dawn, I finished scattering Pookie parts just under the surface of the lawn in the roped-off area where the other funerals would be held. I replaced the final divot and tamped it down, so it wasn't too obviously lumpy. After all, I wanted someone to catch a heel and make the gruesome discovery; I had no intention of making the place look like a charnel house.

On our way back to Sunset Rest, I treated Simon to a well-earned breakfast at Mel's Diner. We dawdled over coffee until I figured that the mourners would have begun to arrive for the funerals. Then I disguised my voice with a napkin and called the *L.A. Times* and *Variety* from the old-fashioned pay phone out front and gleefully tattled on the atrocity taking place at Hollywood Gardens.

Julia Shrike would be, no pun intended, mortified.

The fallout was everything I'd hoped for and more. The California Funeral and Cemetery Bureau swooped down on Julia like a horde of blowflies on an exposed eyeball. I contented myself with a job well done.

Two weeks later, I thrust a fax across Simon's desk.

"This came in last night. On the sly from the Coroner's Office. What do you think?"

Simon looked at it and blinked.

"Coco Chablis?"

Chablis was an R&B artist with several platinum albums, as famous for her music as she was for her drug use and her struggles with obesity. Her notoriety would soar even more as soon as the press found out she'd expired in flagrante delicto with a nineteen-year-old pizza boy who had died at the same time. Except that he had perished of suffocation when he couldn't wriggle out from under her.

"She's ours?" Simon asked, hopefully.

"Not yet. But she's going to be."

Though Coco Chablis wasn't as big a name as Kyle Bee, she was a singer, and the fans of singers tend to be far more devoted to their idols in death. Long after a motion picture celebrity has begun to fade into obscurity, a rock star's tomb will continue to accumulate grave offerings, and their fans will happily pay through the nose to be close to them after death. You see it in life as well, I suppose. Film aficionados collect movie star autographs, while a band's groupies cherish everything from locks of hair, to sweaty T-shirts, to half-eaten muffins and used tissues. Given the choice, I'd take one Michael Jackson over five Elizabeth Taylors any day.

"What about the necrophiliac bitch?"

"Bite your tongue." I warned, and then rubbed my palms together with anticipatory glee.

"I'm going to stuff that oversized musical dumpling into a deluxe satin-lined, double-wide casket from *our* showroom, with all the upgrades and trimmings, and plant her in a premium plot in *my* park before Julia Shrike knows what hit her."

"Why limit ourselves?" A sly smile, holding just enough greed to be interesting, confirmed why I'd always liked him. "How do you think they'd feel about a mausoleum?"

"The heck with how they'd feel. *I'd* love it."

"I could make that pitch," he mused aloud. "A big house for a big talent."

"And a very big girl."

"I think maybe I should skip that part. It might be better to present it as a physical monument to her fame. A Mecca for her fans across the world."

I closed my eyes and inhaled through my nostrils, as if the idea was a fine perfume.

"I can see it now, Simon. We'll set up pilgrimage tours. I'll cut the family a deal on the embalming in exchange for marketing rights. I'm picturing a whole line of officially licensed Coco Chablis memorial wreaths, right next to the coffee mugs, T-shirts and commemorative cremation urns."

Simon's grin widened.

"It so happens," I told him as I grabbed my car keys, "that Howard Horowitz was her manager. And coincidentally," I allowed my grin to match Simon's, "Howard owes me a favor."

I was pleasantly surprised at how easy it was to wrap up the Coco Chablis deal. Every time I dealt with the family I was alert for any trace of the foul stench of Julia Shrike. Yet, to my delight, I had nary a whiff. Not only did we get the funeral and the interment, but Simon proved his worth by getting the family to spring for a huge dog of a mausoleum with space for sixteen caskets that we'd built on spec and hadn't been able to sell. He convinced them that since Coco's estate was footing the bill, it would not only be tax deductible as a promotional expense but, for all practical purposes, fifteen other family members would be getting *their* crypts virtually for free.

As for my contribution to the Sunset Rest Memorial Park's

coffers, I humbly admit I outdid myself. Inspiration struck me while we were going over the arrangements, and Coco's casket ended up not being satin lined after all. I talked them into fur instead, real mink dyed a delicate pink. Her burial gown was several dozen yards of a multi-layered Schiaparelli creation, also in pink, and almost big enough to justify adding a few feet to the custom-made casket. Upon consideration, though, I decided not to push my luck. We would figure a way to cram it all into the one we had and still make it look nice.

The floral tributes were, if I may say so, spectacular. Since orchids were the deceased's favorite flower, I arranged for five hundred rare specimens to be flown in overnight from the Amazon rain forest on a specially chartered plane. Even better, with Howard's help, we managed to get Coco's record label to pick up the tab. The catering for the wake was...well, I can't even begin to describe the extravagance other than to say that, within a week, a few of the canapes that were smuggled out of the event were listed on E-bay, practically petrified by then, with bids approaching five figures.

I was pleased with myself, pleased as punch. So pleased that I forgot the old adage about pride and falls. I was caught completely off guard when, two days before the funeral, Julia Shrike made her next move.

"What is this?"

I stared, puzzled, at the piece of paper Simon handed me.

"An exhumation order," Simon said, dolefully.

"A *what*? For *whom*?"

From the way he avoided making eye contact with me, I knew it had to be bad.

"Victor Reed."

My head snapped back from the shock of it, as if I had sipped from a glass of fine champagne and gotten a mouthful of formaldehyde instead. Reed was a Hollywood legend, one of the few actors from the Golden Age who could eclipse the popularity of modern rock stars. His tomb, located prominently on a low hill rising from the very center of Sunset Rest, was a rococo monument to bad taste. Fifty years after the twenty-seven-year-old Reed met his maker, the mythos surrounding his tragic suicide continued to grow, inspiring new generations of fans to adulation. Twice a month, we scrubbed the marble free of lipstick stains, and collected enough wilted tulips—his signature flower—to pay for Holland's annual windmill budget.

Somehow, by means of some nefarious and hellish scheme, Julia had finagled Reed's grandchildren into exhuming his body and moving it to Hollywood Gardens.

"Reed is our biggest draw," I managed to croak past a throat, tongue, and lips that were suddenly as desiccated as any Egyptian mummy.

"It gets worse," Simon said.

"It can't possibly."

"And yet it does. Take a look at when they're going to do it."

"That's...that's..." I stammered.

Fury battled for prominence over outrage. Outrage eventually won.

"That *fucking bitch*!" I yelled. "That's right in the middle of the Chablis funeral! She can't do this!"

"It's a court order, Mickey. Look on the bright side. At least it's far enough away so that no one will have a clear view of what's happening."

"They're still going to know *something* is going on! You can bet your ass Julia doesn't intend to have it done quietly, with picks and shovels like a normal person. No, that...that...*harridan* will use a backhoe. Just in case that's not disruptive enough, she'll probably hire a fife and drum corps to draw even *more* attention to it."

"Do you need a drink, Mickey?"

"No," I snapped. "I need a hit man. With a pack of trained cobras."

"They might refuse to bite one of their own."

"There's something else, isn't there, Simon? I can tell by your face. What is it?"

He hemmed and hawed, but eventually, he got around to it.

"She's making a documentary about it."

I knew my voice was dangerously low. "A...*what*?"

"Julia announced it on the Hollywood Gardens website. It's all about Victor Reed's career and his...er...detours until he reached his pre-destined resting place..." He paused and then added, "At Hollywood Gardens."

Just in case I missed the point. "Can she do that?"

"How are we going to stop it, Mickey? She'll have a film crew with her. Anything we try will only make it worse. Besides, do we really want to raise a ruckus in front of Coco Chablis's people? If we'd known sooner, maybe we could've gotten a restraining order. But the courts are closed for the weekend."

"This is the last straw. I mean it, Simon. The. Last. Straw."

"Please don't do anything stupid."

"Who? Me? Obviously, you don't know me very well."

"That's the problem, Mickey," Simon said with a heavy sigh. "I *do* know you. That's what I'm afraid of."

The morning of the Chablis funeral dawned clear and bright, one of those perfect California days where the sun is just hot enough to burn away the marine layer without making everyone's antiperspirant completely useless, and the breeze coming from Santa Monica is just strong enough to blow most of the freeway smog toward Riverside County.

Technically, the park wasn't open yet, but when the exhumation crew arrived early, I told Simon to let them in. I didn't want to risk the additional embarrassment of having the backhoe and dump trucks fighting for parking spaces with Chablis's hearse and the limos in the funeral procession.

The funeral would be held in our on-site chapel. At the conclusion of the main service, the mourners would walk down the paths and across the graveyard to reassemble in front of the tomb. We'd rented several hundred comfortable chairs and arranged them in rows beneath large pink canopies to shelter everyone from the sun. We'd also set up banquet tables, festooned with frilly bunding in Coco's signature pink, to display the overflow of floral tributes, and to provide cucumber, mandarin, lemon grass, or mint-infused, organic spring water to help make sure none of the family, Coco's colleagues from the music industry, or the fans who won tickets to the funeral in the online contests would become too dehydrated from weeping.

While everyone was settling in, a specially commissioned pink hearse would transport Coco's casket from the chapel to the graveside, where it would be unloaded onto a display trestle designed specifically to support the weight. I had a team of self-proclaimed designers from one of the HGTV improvement shows ready to spring into action and arrange even more pink roses, carnations, and other flowers around the coffin so that the guests would have something pretty to look at during the additional hour or so of tributes.

I'd have to maintain a properly respectful visage, and some-how refrain from yawning, until the last of Coco's colleagues and fans finished what promised to be a virtually endless litany of eulogies and memorial anecdotes. Once the speakers wound down, the pallbearers would carry Coco into the mausoleum where I would make sure they slid her into the proper slot, and that the workers did a good job affixing the marble front and screwing the nameplate into place. Then I'd lock the tomb and rush off to the wake, where I'd share a few toasts to the dearly departed and present the final bill to Howard Horowitz for payment.

I was alone in the chapel, contemplating that happy thought, and fussing with the wreaths, when the evil bitch cornered me.

"A bit over-the-top, wouldn't you say? At Hollywood Gardens, we pride ourselves on tastefulness."

"I thought you prided yourself on vitriol."

"Oh, I save all of that for you, Mickey, my dear," she said with a crystalline laugh.

I hadn't actually seen Julia, in person, in a couple of years.

Much to my chagrin, she didn't seem to have aged at all. I'd have been pleased to see a few wrinkles, a slight sag to the chin, some facial scarring, or perhaps even a missing limb or three. Unfortunately, she was just as ravishing as always and, though I hated her like the poison I so badly wished someone would slip into her morning coffee, I couldn't help feeling the ghostly pull of that same erotic sensuality that I hadn't been able to resist as a teenager.

"I'd have thought you'd be out on the lawn, Micky. Bidding goodbye to your old friend, Victor Reed."

"Well, we'll be sorry to see him go."

I kept my tone light and casual. I'd throw myself into my own crematorium before I'd give her any outward signs of how badly her latest machination had damaged us. It was hard to believe this tiny, gorgeous creature was the closest thing on earth to a minion of Hell.

"You're taking this far better than I expected," she said with a scowl of disappointment.

I shrugged. "What's to be done about it? You've always done your worst, and I'm still surviving. Besides, there's always a bright side."

"Oh, really?" she asked with insincere sweetness. "What's that?"

"*We* had Victor Reed while he was still *fresh*," I said, solemnly. "You can never take that away."

"Maybe not," she agreed, and her smile compared unfavorably with the expression on the face of a particularly gruesome burn victim I'd once embalmed.

"But you can bet your ass I intend to dig up or disinter every other celebrity you've got. Down to the last god-damned bit player. By the time I'm finished with you, Mickey Baxter, you'll be selling plots in bulk to illegal immigrants for twenty pesos and a free photograph with the zebra-striped mule."

Her overt threat was, I suppose, the thing that finally set me off. I wanted to wipe the smirk off her face with the help of a

137

nearby pew. But I would be damned if I'd let Julia see how badly she'd gotten under my skin. I pretended to adjust the wreath again while I summoned my control and, when I finally spoke, I was surprised by how level my voice was.

"You are vile," was all I said to her. "Truly vile."

I refused to allow her the satisfaction of a response. I turned on my heel and strode off to make some final preparations for the Chablis send-off.

As the deceased woman's business manager, Howard was granted the honor of giving the final eulogy. Once he wrapped it up, I mounted the little dais and officially invited everyone to share the buffet and hosted bar at the wake. As the crowd slowly filtered across the lawn toward the reception hall, the eight pall bearers hoisted the coffin and bore it into the mausoleum. I felt for them, laboring with their burden as they did.

Coco Chablis was, indeed, a big girl. After all, it took quite a bit of heft to belt out a number like she did.

Julia Shrike, on the other hand, barely displaced the Schiaparelli ruffles.

I was sure they'd be quite comfy together.

CHRISTINE THIRTEEN

Melinda Loomis

I grew up in a lesser part of Santa Monica back when Southern California still had beach communities that weren't overbuilt and overpriced. I spent most of my days at the beach in the California sun. It was a pretty carefree existence, back before I learned what a cruel place the world could be.

I had a pretty happy and unremarkable life until I hit my teens. The problem with teenage girls is that they think they're grown up when they're not even close and think they know it all when they don't. I was typical in that regard. I was also what my mother politely referred to as an "early developer," so I looked more mature than I really was, and that only fed into my belief that I was more of a young woman than a girl.

I was thirteen when Danny Strauss came into my young life.

He was the gardener and handyman at our apartment building. He had a sun-streaked lion's mane, sparkling sea-blue eyes, and a California tan. He went simply by "Strauss." In my young eyes, he was a one-named, sapphire-eyed surfer god.

All he had to do was send an acknowledging nod my way and my day was made. When he spoke to me, I walked on air. I fantasized innocently about being his girlfriend, age difference be damned. After all, I *felt* grown up.

One day he waved me over and handed me a dollar bill. Only

one, but money was tight in my family, and I didn't get a regular allowance, so to me it was a small fortune. Plus, it was from Strauss, passed from his large, sun-kissed hand to my pudgy paw, so it was special. I was at a besotted loss for how to form an intelligent response or even a simple thank you. Strauss bestowed an understanding smile on me and said the gift was because I was a good kid and "not like those screaming brats downstairs who tear the place up." He meant the Logan monsters, as my parents referred to them. They were loud and obnoxious, and their parents didn't seem to care who they bothered or what they damaged. I was a good girl, not a Logan, and Strauss had noticed. I was in heaven.

I ran upstairs clutching my treasure and burst through the door. In an elated daze, I waved the dollar at my mom, who was parked on the couch watching a soap opera.

"Mom, look!"

She bolted up from the couch. "Where did you get that?"

I was shocked by her reaction. Did she think I stole it? What had I ever done to make her think I'd steal money?

"Strauss gave it to me," I explained, confident that would set everything straight.

It didn't.

"Christine Mariah," she admonished, complete with middle name so I'd know how grave my unintentional transgression had been, "you know better. I thought you were smarter than that, taking money from a stranger. God knows what he'll want in return."

I didn't care for her ugly insinuation. "He's not a stranger," I pointed out. "He works here."

She wasn't swayed. "He's been here maybe a month and we hardly know him."

Then she took my dollar. My precious dollar that was a gift from Strauss.

"He said it was because I was good, not like the Logan monsters," I whined, but she wasn't interested.

Mom marched me downstairs to where Strauss was hosing off the driveway, and with me cringing at her side proceeded to ream him for giving money to a child he barely knew. I'm not sure what was more mortifying—that she was making a scene in front of Strauss, or that she described me as a child. I didn't feel like a child and I certainly didn't want Strauss to view me as such.

The poor guy was stunned and stuttered that he hadn't meant any harm, just thought it would be a nice thing to do since I was a good kid. "I'm really sorry," he told Mom meekly. "The ice cream truck should be around later, and I thought it would be nice for Christine to have a treat."

The truck was in fact due, and my mom wilted a bit under his horrified reaction and innocent explanation. But she made him take the dollar back, lectured him that it looked bad for a guy his age to be giving money to a kid, and didn't let me get ice cream that day just to drive the point home.

"I want to make sure you actually learn from this. You won't if you get a popsicle."

I resented her for days, not so much about the ice cream, but for making Strauss feel bad and for embarrassing me in front of him. I thought she'd made a big deal out of nothing and it pissed me off.

I did learn from the experience, just not the way Mom had hoped. The next time Strauss gave me a dollar for ice cream, all sneaky-like this time, I didn't tell her. It was our secret, he explained, and I was happy to play along. I kept this dollar hidden, safe from her, until one day she wasn't around when the ice cream truck drove by, and I triumphantly busted it out and had an orange Creamsicle, courtesy of the living god that was Strauss.

The third time Strauss gave me money it was a ten, and I learned two things the hard way: I should have listened to Mom, and I wasn't as grown up as I'd thought.

* * *

A few weeks after Strauss gave me ten dollars and took something from me that you couldn't put a price on, I listened in horror as Mom placed a call to the apartment manager. The garbage disposal had just given up the ghost, so could he please send Strauss over with a replacement? I was mortified at having to face him in my own home, a place where I should have been able to feel safe from him. I'd been spending a lot of time inside lately, something my parents didn't seem to have noticed.

But when the new disposal arrived, a new handyman came with it. He was an older guy named Jenkins who was very polite to my mom and barely seemed to notice me at all.

We learned from Jenkins that Strauss had just left for a better job. So that was going to be it? No accountability, no one swooping in to avenge what he'd done to me? He had just walked away, out into the world, without so much as a slap on the wrist.

I partially blamed myself, as victims often do, for not saying anything at the time. There was a perverse part of me that was still beholden to my crush on Strauss, not to mention the embarrassment and potential stigma of what had happened between us. When I would occasionally consider mentioning it, I'd freeze up both physically and emotionally. My parents attributed my personality changes to my being a teenager, because, as I learned, I was at what parents refer to as "a difficult age."

So I kept my secret, the one that ate at my soul and tormented my dreams.

Thanks to Strauss, I really didn't have much of a life.

I spent my teen years being secretive and churlish. No one read much into it. The teenage-phase thing again. Growing into adulthood I had no ambition. Nothing seemed to matter or inspire any real interest. I obsessed about Strauss and the very adult things he had done to me when I was only thirteen. Do I even need to mention my inability to form functional adult relationships?

I finished high school without distinguishing myself and embarked on several meaningless office jobs that barely covered my bills and didn't contribute a thing toward filling the hole in my soul.

The years didn't dim Strauss. He was a regular participant in my chronic nightmares. In my dreams I tried to rearrange what had happened so that it put us on equal footing, so I could somehow rationalize it, but to no avail. He was always the victor and I was always the victim. I didn't need an expert to analyze my dreams. I was still being victimized. What Strauss had done to me was imprinted on my psyche and wouldn't go away.

I also freak out mentally whenever someone hands me a ten-dollar bill. To this day, the simple act of receiving change for a twenty hurtles me right back to that day when Strauss handed me a ten and I thought he was just being really nice.

At some point I started wondering if he was still alive. Maybe he'd given a couple bucks to the wrong person's kid. Maybe they'd called the cops and he was in prison, preferably with a three-hundred-pound cellmate named Bubba, or maybe they'd just dealt with him man to man. These possibilities strangely saddened me.

Because I wanted to be the one to make him pay. I fantasized about finding him and killing him all the damn time.

I found him on my birthday.

I'd bought a cake and a bottle of wine, and that was the extent of my celebrating a day that no longer meant anything to me. I got a call from my parents, who had recently moved to Las Vegas because the cost of living has gotten so out of hand here in Southern California. The days of people like us living by the beach are long gone. They seem to like it there, had even been able to finally buy a place of their own instead of renting. We made small talk and hung up. A part of me had always blamed them for not somehow figuring out how I had come to be so damaged, and our relationship never recovered.

I poured myself a glass of wine, cut a huge slab of cake, and parked myself in front of my laptop. It dawned on me now that I was twenty-six, and that meant it had been thirteen years since Strauss had violated me at thirteen. Double the bad luck, and I decided then and there that I had waited long enough. No more fantasizing—it was time for action.

I searched the name "Daniel Strauss" with "Santa Monica" and found that it was, as I'd expected, a pretty common name. This was going to take a while, which was fine by me. I had nothing but time.

About a half hour into my search, I clicked on a link to *The Argonaut*, a free paper that covers Santa Monica and the surrounding beach cities. It was a small article, about nine months old, that said police had arrested a suspect who had been pestering area kids, specifically girls in their early teens. He was identified as Daniel Stephen Strauss, whose residence was a homeless encampment at Venice Beach.

I kept searching until I finally found a mug shot and nearly had a stroke—I was looking into those striking blue eyes once again. Even in a black and white photo, they were still electrifying. It was definitely him. Even thirteen years older and looking very much the worse for wear, the eyes gave him away.

I ran to the bathroom, threw up my wine and cake, then returned to my laptop to review research I'd already gone over countless times before. It was time to act. It was time for payback.

I started taking coffee to homeless people in Venice in the evenings after work. It's cold at night at the beach.

I told people I was doing it because I didn't feel like I was contributing anything to the world and just wanted to help in some small way. Of course, that wasn't true. I was hunting for

Strauss.

I would make pots of coffee and fill dozens of cups. I bought Styrofoam cups with plastic lids in bulk at Walmart. Half of the coffees would be black, the other half cream and sugar. Then the lids went on and were numbered—even for black, odd for cream and sugar—and off I went to bring a little sliver of warmth into the lives of the less fortunate.

Two cups—one black, one with cream and sugar, both numbered thirteen—got an additional ingredient. Those were never handed out. They were special orders, waiting for a special someone.

Over the past thirteen years, not only had I imagined exacting revenge on Strauss, but I'd also figured out how I'd do it, given the opportunity. Shooting was briefly considered but got a pass because it's loud and attracts attention, and I had no intention of getting caught. I was already serving a life sentence; I wasn't about to serve another one.

I had also considered antifreeze, which was the poison of choice on some true crime shows I'd seen. Heck, you can get it at Walmart—just another item in a basket filled with all kinds of normal stuff, which I considered a good thing because I was unlikely to be remembered out of the mass of people who go through there, as opposed to a chick clearly out of her element at the local Pep Boys.

What made antifreeze so popular was its sweet taste, enabling it to be hidden in all kinds of food and drinks. But the people who used antifreeze always seemed to get caught. I also wasn't sure I could get a lethal dose in one beverage and there was the possibility Strauss might not want his coffee sweetened, so I discarded that option.

The internet is a wonderful thing. As I researched poisons, I found that it's pretty amazing—and kind of disturbing—how easy it is to find deadly materials that are perfectly legal to own, mostly plants. This seemed more doable, except for the part where I'm lousy with plants and I'd probably kill it before I got a chance to use it to kill Strauss. But I stumbled across another option: pure nicotine. And it was readily available wherever e-cigarettes and their cartridges were sold.

I had to poke around a few sites to find out if it was too good to be true. But no, I could easily buy pure nicotine. One site selling it even had a huge warning that it was "poison in its raw form" and had to be handled properly. Message received, but probably not the one they were trying to send.

I also learned that nicotine has a predictably tarry taste but could be masked with flavoring. Luckily, e-cigs were available in a variety of flavors, some fruity, some minty; even bubblegum was an option. And they say they're not trying to pawn this stuff off on kids. Yeah, right.

Another option? Coffee flavor.

Forty milligrams was a lethal dose, but I bought a lot more than that. I bought everything else that went with it and began vaping, so if anyone asked, I'd have an alibi for my purchases.

It was a Tuesday night when all my research, planning and philanthropy finally paid off. A little over a month into my charity work, a homeless guy with what had once been dazzling blue eyes shuffled over to the short line to reap the benefits of my generosity. When we were face to face, I knew I'd found him.

I'd envisioned this moment countless times and always feared I'd panic and bolt. But I didn't. In fact, I felt eerily serene. I took that as proof that my mission was righteous.

I smiled at him and calmly said, "Hi, Strauss."

He looked at me with a combination of surprise and suspicion but didn't seem to be able to place me.

"It's me," I told him, "Christine from Santa Monica. That crappy old apartment building on Ashland."

He simply stared. I plowed on.

"You worked there for a little while. And I don't believe for a second that you don't remember me, although I probably wasn't the only kid you gave ten bucks to."

That did it. He started to shake uncontrollably and then emitted weird, choking sobs. I found this deeply satisfying.

"Strauss," I lied, "I want you to know something. I forgive you."

He looked at me with watery blue eyes for a few seconds, then finally spoke, so softly I could barely hear him. "God bless you," he murmured. "I'm so sorry. I'm so sorry."

Yeah, I thought. *You're* sorry. You're sorry now. That doesn't erase the last thirteen years, and some things are unforgiveable.

But outwardly I nodded, smiling benevolently, then asked him, "Strauss, do you take your coffee black or with cream and sugar?"

"Cream and sugar," came the miserable reply. I gave him a cup numbered thirteen.

He took it with a trembling hand, nodded helplessly, and ambled over to the curb. He plopped down, leaning against a light post, a sad excuse for a man wrapped in a ratty blanket. Then he began sipping his coffee. Even now, it still didn't bother him to take from me.

I never took my eyes off him. It took him about five minutes to finish the drink. And at that dose, it only took a few more minutes for him to stop shifting under the blanket.

I'm not sorry, and I don't feel the least bit guilty. He brought it on himself. He did the crime, and I finally made him do the time. He'll never touch another kid.

Now the homeless guy I used as a guinea pig when I first started serving coffee, to make sure the nicotine OD would really work? That guy I do feel bad about.

EPILOGUE

On the day after Thanksgiving 2020 the editors of *Avenging Angelenos* Sarah M. Chen, Pamela Samuels Young, and Wrona Gall met with Sisters in Crime Los Angeles's "House Arrest" host and writer August Norman over videoconference to chat about their experiences writing, editing and working together in the middle of the strangest year in living memory. This is a lightly edited transcript of their conversation.

AN: August Norman
PSY: Pamela Samuels Young
WG: Wrona Gall
SMC: Sarah M. Chen

AN: Welcome to the epilogue conversation of the 2021 Sisters in Crime Los Angeles anthology *Avenging Angelenos*. We're here to talk with the co-editors about the work it takes to put something like this all together.

With me, of course, are Sarah Chen, Pamela Samuels Young, and Wrona Gall. Let's take a second and meet each of you. Sarah Chen, let's talk about your background as a writer as well as what made you want to be an editor of an anthology.

SMC: I am mostly a crime fiction short story writer. I wrote a novella *Cleaning Up Finn* and also a children's chapter book. I tend to gravitate toward the shorter works and I've co-edited two anthologies so I really was excited when I was asked to be an editor for the Sisters in Crime anthology. I love short stories and crime fiction and Sisters in Crime.

AN: Pamela, same question. Tell us how you got involved.

PSY: I got an email and I was really excited! It was particularly special for me because my first published short story was in *Landmarked for Murder* which was a SINC anthology published in 2003 or 2004. And when I got that notification that I was in *Landmarked for Murder*, I had just, a few months before, gotten my first agent after months of rejection so it was like okay, now it's going to happen. Oprah's going to be calling me any day. It's God. So that was particularly special for me. And I write legal thrillers. I'm a lawyer, retired in 2016 to write full-time. I had all these plans to publish two or three books a year in retirement and I actually wrote more when I was working.

AN: Wrona, same question to you.

WG: Actually I just had two short stories published but when I was accepted into...what was our...? Sarah, I can't remember the name of ours.

SMC: Was it *Ladies Night* or was it *LAst Resort*?

WG: *LAst Resort*. Okay. Thank you. So, when I got published in that, it was a few months after I'd moved here so it was really significant, making me feel at home and welcome. I also think Sisters in Crime is a great group and I did feel really honored to edit as a way of giving back. I like the editing process since it's like painting; each refinement improves the work.

AN: Let's talk specifically about this anthology *Avenging Angelenos*. The Sisters in Crime Los Angeles Chapter Anthology Committee put together a list of qualifications. Each story that would be considered would a) have a word count under 7500 words b) touch on the theme of *Avenging Angelenos*: "Sometimes revenge is the only option for what's gotten under the skin," c) be set within or around Los Angeles County and d) incorporate a capital or major crime such as murder (or something very bad.) These themes become the undercurrents of crime that work their way through all eleven selected stories.

Let's talk a little bit about the fun of that idea of Los Angeles as a place that needs revenge or avenging. Whoever wants to start...

PSY: I think L.A.'s a great setting for stories, revenge, murder, whatever. All of my novels, I have fourteen, take place in the Los Angeles area. And every year, I say I'm going to study another city and write something else. But I always write about L.A. One, it's safe because I know L.A., but also there are so many places, so many landmarks that you can write about. So that's my two cents on that.

SMC: And L.A. has so many different communities. So many little neighborhoods where I feel like revenge is done in different ways depending on where you are from. If you're from the beach area, you may plot revenge one way versus someone who lives in a more urban area, or downtown. So I feel like that theme really utilizes the diversity of the various L.A. microcosms.

AN: Wrona, do you have anything on this one?

WG: Well, I think also, based on what Sarah said, revenge is very personal. I've never had any *big time* revenge experiences, but if I think about it...there's that girl in grade school who squirted me with a hose and I still remember her name and...

PSY: *[laughs]*

WG: ...I plan to kill her off one day. *[smiles]*
I think cities are exciting. I happen to live in Ojai and I really miss the city because of the vibrancy and the different personalities and I like all those things. I think L.A. is an exciting city to base the Anthology in.

AN: Obviously, the years 2020 and 2021 when this anthology will be published have been unlike anything in our recent history with the presence of a pandemic. Each contributor submitted something in the middle of an uncertain time, then you all volunteered to select and edit these stories, also in bizarre times. What's it like to be creative in the middle of a pandemic, first of all, not to mention broad civil unrest? How did the epic changes in the world around us impact the creative processes for both the authors in the stories that came through and for yourselves?

WG: Well, I actually was very happy to have a distraction from the political reality we've had in the last four years so it was really nice not to have to think of anything and to be in control of something that would have a positive outcome. That felt really good to me. What was the second part? [laughs]

AN: Did it change the stories at all?

WG: It probably influenced the stories but personally my experience has been very positive. Eliminating so many social things allowed me to have my time in my studio as well as writing and so that was a positive. I live in Ojai which is really a tiny oasis so I am fortunate not to have lost anyone but I wish there was more I could do to help so many besides offering support.

PSY: I'll say it impacted me a lot. I didn't really feel like writing and there were times when I would turn on cable news, promising that I was just going to get the gist of what's happening today and turn it off and then three or four hours later, I'm still there, and I'm feeling not great about what I'm seeing and shocked and all those things and it just sort of bothered me.

And I'm an early morning writer so if I don't get up at six or so to write, it is rare that I would go back to the computer after eight or nine. I can outline and do other things throughout the day or night but the creative process has to be in the morning for me.

But I did discover something great along the way because if I'm writing in the morning, then I'm not exercising. If I'm exercising, then I'm not writing. And I'm definitely a morning person.

But I discovered "Otter", a dictation app. So I now walk and dictate a chapter or two and have the app transcribes it and I edit it from there.

And the pandemic has affected me. One of my closest friends just got out of the hospital and he's still on oxygen and I have people who lost parents. Luckily, my family's fine but it's real and it has impacted me.

SMC: Yeah, for me it was really hard. In the beginning, I couldn't write. I couldn't even read fiction. I was just reading news headlines and I was glued to CNN and just anything I could read about the virus. My dad lives in Taiwan, and I was worried about him initially when it wasn't over here yet. And he was traveling and so I was an anxious, neurotic mess. I had a friend who passed away but I wasn't sure if it was complications from COVID or not.

But then I started writing essays to work through my feelings and then I just thought, you know, as a writer that's kind of how we work through things and how we connect with people. I felt so isolated. So eventually I started to get back into writing as thinking of it as, okay, this is the way I process everything. This is the way I try to connect with the world. But it took me at least four or five months to write.

AN: The selection of an anthology takes several months as well. What was it like to select stories for an anthology? What appeals to you specifically or generally? And did the times influence those selections at all or was it again, sort of as Wrona said, more of an escape to lose yourself in someone else's fiction?

What was it like to judge other authors' work and to find the jewels among them?

PSY: I thought it was pretty interesting because when we all came together, there were some that we agreed on and there were others that might be one of my favorites, but might not have been somebody else's favorite and vice versa. I tend to like the mystery, legal mystery, the murder and mayhem, and there were some things I typically wouldn't read but there were stories that I actually kind of fell in love with. And one pretty quirky story that I thought was particularly well-written that I really liked a lot. And it wouldn't have been something that I normally bought if I saw it on the bookshelf but now maybe I might.

AN: Same question, Wrona.

WG: I agree. It was interesting how some popped up to the top right away. Those are definite choices. Then it was very interesting as you read through and you were trying to evaluate and prioritize the other ones. I had a little difficulty with some genres, such as supernatural. Editing such a story was a little harder challenge for me. But it was just like Pamela said, it was very interesting that you just had to open your eyes to something else and it became more exciting. There's one new author who will be initially published in the anthology. She was completely professional. Had everything lined up perfectly. It was exciting to see that somebody new was going to be published. We editors also have had the benefit of being published in a SinCLA anthology and could pay it forward. A good experience.

AN: Great, and Sarah?

SMC: It was a really fun process. I feel like we all came into agreement as far as what stories we wanted to choose and it was pretty seamless as far as who wanted what stories to edit. I also found myself drawn to stories that normally I don't usually gravitate to so I thought that was interesting. It opened up my appreciation for a different, maybe a supernatural story. I feel like it enriched my reading tastes.

AN: There's part of being an editor that is also giving an author perhaps their first break. Sarah, having edited multiple anthologies, would you talk about the honor of that and the excitement of discovering something new?

SMC: I remember I was so excited when my short story was selected for Sisters in Crime, the *Ladies Night* anthology. And I cannot remember what year that was. 2013? I submitted every year before that to Sisters in Crime. It was always my goal to get into an anthology and I always got rejected but I kept trying. It was so nice to have the whole chapter support me and there was a wonderful launch party. So to give back and be able to do that for other writers is really rewarding. It's a big deal, especially if it's their first publication.

AN: And we do have one first publication in this anthology?

WG: Yes, the writer I mentioned.

PSY: I think one of mine is a first.

AN: Pamela, since you're on camera, tell us the same thing. What's that experience like? The honor of discovering?

PSY: It was nice. It was also nice working with the authors. It made me remember how I was as a first-time author. Because I remember after my first book deal getting that editor's letter and seeing all the changes that she wanted and freaking out and thinking my writing life was going to be over and they were awful changes. But knowing what I know now ...

One particular change that I'll never forget, that an editor wanted me to make, was the ending. And for at least a couple weeks I walked around the house moaning but when I finally decided to write it the way the editor wanted me to write it, I realized she was right on the money.

But that also taught me about that inner writing process because when I first started editing the short stories, I was really heavy-handed. And then I went back and changed just stylistic things. Because if I had gotten that as a first-time author, I would have freaked out. So I went back and I was more tempered in the changes that I made and through discussion and back and forth, we went through the process.

So it also made me remember how I felt as a new author and even now as an author when I get critiques because I have a very set focus group and I listen to what they say and I look for things that are in common. So it made me better. I think it'll make me a better writer in terms of getting critiqued myself.

AN: Wrona? Same question.

WG: I forgot the question. [laughs]

AN: What is it like working with these authors, sometimes new authors, editing someone else's material and the honor and discovery of that sort of responsibility?

WG: Thank you. I'm actually a painter by profession and you achieve a more exciting image when you can apply information from a critique. I always think of it (editing) as a very positive experience.

Now the newest author I worked with was very happy to have any changes made. Then the person who has published quite a bit said "oh yes, I'm sure you have a good opinion. It sounds good. Do it." And then another writer and I needed to speak in person to communicate our thoughts. Another writer and I needed to speak in person to communicate our thoughts.

Once we were zooming the ideas flowed and I believe we were both satisfied with the process. I think Sarah mentioned working with others in groups can be challenging but discussing comments in person or in zoom clarifies everything. Zoom meetings are starting to feel like real life!

AN: Because of the pandemic you were restricted from actually sitting with the authors or the other editors in person. How were you able to collaborate with the authors and with each other? Zoom? FaceTime? Wrona?

WG: With the other editors it was basically on Zoom. It's extremely challenging for me because I almost a couple times screamed "Jim!" because my husband will just hop on these things for me. I'm a total non-tech. I type with two fingers.

So basically, it was more challenging. I would've loved the in-person at a coffee shop. It's much more natural for me. I would've been happy to come down to L.A. just for that benefit but it's the reality of what we have and as you get used to this, you realize well, there are some good points of convenience like saving time but I do think the visual is very important. At least for me. If it wasn't a Zoom, if it was just a phone call, it would've been more difficult.

AN: Pamela, same?

PSY: All of my communications (with the story authors) were via email except for one author that we talked a couple times by phone. And I think it was very helpful to talk by phone. Because the other authors were all published and we were pretty straightforward. There were some things that with one of the writers that I suggested that weren't particularly their style and that was fine. But there was never anything that there was ultimately a disagreement on. We all I think, worked well.

AN: And Sarah, same question.

SMC: All the authors had been published before so it was pretty smooth. Just strictly email back and forth. I couldn't have asked for better writers.

AN: These anthologies are a great way to discover new talent, to showcase other talent, to allow authors who might normally write in novel length fiction to try something new in a short story. Is there a last thought as we look at this anthology and future anthologies? Something that might guide other Sisters in Crime authors who want to appear in these anthologies as they go forward with the next bit?

SMC: I think if you're considering submitting to the Sisters in Crime anthology or any anthology that draws you in then definitely submit. It's exciting when you're selected!

I really hope we can do something fun and exciting in 2021 when we launch this. However, that may be a virtual bookstore launch—hopefully we'll be able to do something in person. If it's not on the publication date, maybe later in the year, we'll get together and see people. That would be fantastic, so that's what I truly hope for all these writers.

AN: Wrona, last thoughts?

WG: Just like Sarah said, I remember the launch party. It was just so exciting. And for me when I went to book conferences, I was so impressed, like "oh my god, that's so and so." I mean actors, eh, no big deal, but it was so exciting to think of these writers—I read their words, they've entertained me. Conferences and meetings provide this wonderful enthusiasm that keeps you writing. It's such a validation of all the time and energy we devote to our writing.

AN: And Pamela?

PSY: For people considering submitting to another SinCLA anthology, I would encourage people to study your craft. Which is not what I did when I was starting out writing.

Things did not begin to happen for me until I began to do that. Really. Because you know I sat down and "Oh, I'm a lawyer. I read a lot. I can write a short story. I can write a novel." And that's when all the rejection was at its highest.

Not that it's not going to happen later. You want to write a short story? Read a lot of short stories. You want to write a novel? Read a lot of novels. Study the craft. Things did not happen for me until I began to do that.

Anthologies are exciting. I was accepted into another anthology that has been delayed because of the pandemic and I saw an email a month ago about another anthology that I'm probably going to submit. It's due in January. I haven't started yet but after this discussion, I think I'm actually going to sit down and write something. *[laughs]*

SMC: Yay!

AN: That's probably the best advice to everyone who was either published in this or wants to be published again, don't forget to just do the main job and write. Keep writing and let the world turn you down. Never yourself.

Thank you so much for your contributions to the Anthology. Thank you so much for being here today. We look forward to all getting together, reading and hearing these pieces read out loud as well as just getting to know each other. Thank you so much for editing *Avenging Angelenos*.

[recording ends]

ABOUT THE INTRODUCTION

FRANKIE Y. BAILEY is a criminal justice professor who writes non-fiction about crime history, and crime and mass media/popular culture. Her crime fiction features crime historian Lizzie Stuart and police detective Hannah McCabe. Frankie is a past EVP of Mystery Writers of America and a past president of Sisters in Crime National.

ABOUT THE EDITORS

SARAH M. CHEN has published numerous short stories and a children's book. Her noir novella, *Cleaning Up Finn,* was an Anthony finalist and IPPY Award winner. She is the co-editor, along with E.A. Aymar, of two novel-in-stories, *The Swamp Killers* and *The Night of the Flood*. She's written for the *Los Angeles Review of Books, Hapa Mag, Wellbeing,* and *P.S. I Love You,* among others.

WRONA GALL spent much of her career as a sculptor and painter in a 7000 square foot studio loft in a gritty Chicago neighborhood near her bookie father-in-law. His interesting friends and customers planted the seeds for her fictional characters' lifestyles. A winner of the Malice Domestic Unpublished Writer's Grant, her short stories, "My Beloved" and "Thump, Dump and Bump," were published in the *Fire to Fly* anthology and the 2019 Sisters in Crime Los Angeles anthology, *LAst Resort*. She has written articles for Guppies Sisters in Crime and

Chicago Life Magazine, and served as a panelist at the California Crime Writers and Left Coast Crime conferences.

Attorney and award-winning author **PAMELA SAMUELS YOUNG** writes fast-paced legal thrillers that tackle important social issues. Her novel, *Anybody's Daughter,* which won the NAACP Image Award for Outstanding Fiction, provides an eye-opening look into the world of child sex trafficking. Her latest legal thriller, *Failure to Protect,* takes on the bullying epidemic and its devastating aftermath. The prolific author of more than a dozen books also writes dangerously sexy romantic suspense under the pen name Sassy Sinclair.

Originally from central Indiana, thriller and mystery author and *Avenging Angelenos* Epilogue Host **AUGUST NORMAN** has called Los Angeles home for two decades, writing for and/or appearing in movies, television, stage productions, web series, and even commercial advertising. *Come and Get Me,* August's debut thriller featuring investigative journalist Caitlin Bergman, was listed in *Suspense Magazine*'s "Best of 2019" issue in the debut category and *Sins of the Mother,* the second in the Caitlin Bergman series, was released in September 2020 by Crooked Lane Books.

ABOUT THE CONTRIBUTORS

AVRIL ADAMS lives in the Inland Empire. She writes crime fiction, often in the noir genre. Her story, "The Lowriders," was included in *Last Exit to Murder,* and her story, "Independence Day," was included in *LAst Resort.* She has had several other short stories published. In addition to crime fiction Avril writes science fiction with a humanist twist and children's stories. She is working on a novel starring an African-American, female PI. Her animals are an inspiration for her fiction.

PAULA BERNSTEIN is a New York native, who migrated to California to attend graduate school at Caltech. After several years of work as a chemist, she escaped her laboratory and went to medical school. Like her series heroine, Hannah Kline, Paula spent her professional life practicing Obstetrics and Gynecology in Los Angeles. When she retired from her full-time practice, she reinvented herself as a writer of medical mysteries. She is the author of the Hannah Kline Mysteries. Her short story, "On Call for Murder," was published in the 2017 Sisters in Crime anthology, *LAst Resort.*

Multiple Bram Stoker nominee **HAL BODNER** is best known for his horror comedies and mysteries. His vampire novel, *Bite Club,* was one of the country's bestselling gay novels. He has written several paranormal, erotic romances, and is currently working on a series of thrillers that paint classic noir with a distinctly lavender glaze. His superhero fantasy series debuts in 2021 with *Fabulous in Tights,* followed by *A Study in Spandex,* both from Crossroad Press. He is married to a wonderful man, half his age, who never realized that Liza Minnelli was Judy Garland's daughter.

JENNY CARLESS began her writing career in environmental nonfiction and moved into corporate communications for Silicon Valley clients before tackling fiction. She loves wildlife, photography and travel—particularly into the African bush, which is the inspiration for most of her fiction. For this story, she decided to explore the wildlife in Los Angeles County.

L.H. DILLMAN is not a Brit but a Californian through-and-through, an Angeleno by way of San Francisco, Marin and Napa. Though her law practice focused on business litigation, her early pro bono experiences helping incarcerated individuals fueled an enduring interest in criminal justice. She's the author of four published short stories and is working on a novel involving the wrongful conviction of a Black Panther during the fraught counter-culture era.

GAY TOLTL KINMAN has nine award nominations for her writing. She has published several short stories in American and English magazines and anthologies; twelve children's books and stories; a young-adult gothic novel; eight adult mysteries; and collections of short stories. Several of her short plays were produced—now in a collection of twenty plays, *The Play's the Thing*. She has had many articles published in professional journals and newspapers and has co-edited two non-fiction books. Kinman has library and law degrees.

MELINDA LOOMIS was born and raised in Southern California. She has at times been an office drone (working in everything from insurance to post-production), a culinary student, and an unemployed bum. Her work has appeared in anthologies from the Los Angeles and San Diego Chapters of Sisters in Crime. Melinda lives in Southern California with her extremely photogenic cat Sophie. Visit her online at MelindaLoomis.com.

Bureaucrat by day, author by night, **KATHY NORRIS** has spent more years than she cares to divulge working on the next Great American Novel. Writing "The Ink Well," her short story entry to *Avenging Angelenos*, was a delightful antidote. Kathy has kept her sanity during the pandemic by practicing not-so-hot yoga at home and learning how to operate her iPhone 12.

PEGGY ROTHSCHILD grew up in Los Angeles. Always a mystery-lover, she embraced the tales of Nancy Drew and the Hardy Boys before graduating to the adult section of the library. An English major in high school, she switched to art—her other passion—in college. Peggy's short story, "The Cookie Crumbles," appeared in *The Best Laid Plans: 21 Stories of Mystery & Suspense*. Peggy has also authored two adult mysteries, *Clementine's Shadow* and *Erasing Ramona*, and one young-adult adventure, *Punishment Summer*. Find her at PeggyRothschild.net.

MEREDITH TAYLOR has been in love with mysteries, books and libraries for as long as she can remember. Curiosity about people came next and led to a career. Meredith completed a Ph.D. in clinical psychology at Michigan State University. Without planning it, she worked in levels of care from inpatient to private practice, finishing in a community clinic in beautiful Pasadena, California. In retirement Meredith is penning the adventures of Ali Marchant, therapist and psych professor in Madison, Wisconsin in the 1980s. Through an astonishing coincidence, Meredith lived there at the time. A twelve-year member of Sisters in Crime Los Angeles, Meredith was a board member from 2017-2019.

A third-generation Southern California native, **LAUREL WETZORK** divides her time between writing, consulting, and teaching. Her fiction work is usually set during WWII or in the future, with murder and crime involved, of course. She received her B.A. and master's degrees from the University of Southern California. She and her husband have two cats, enjoy bike-touring, hiking, cooking, and visits from daughter Karina.

BOOKS

On the following pages are a few
more great titles from the
Down & Out Books publishing family.

For a complete list of books and to
sign up for our newsletter,
go to DownAndOutBooks.com.

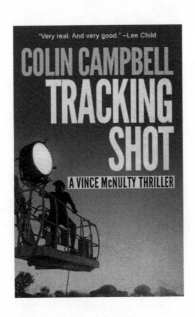

Tracking Shot
A Vince McNulty Thriller
Colin Campbell

Down & Out Books
April 2021
978-1-64396-183-5

Several people are killed when a gunman opens fire while Titanic Productions is filming on a courthouse set in Waltham, MA. Did the gunman mistake the set for the real courthouse down the road? Or was it just a message to the real judge?

When the production is shut down, Larry Unger realizes that secondary footage and the cameraman is missing and Vince McNulty must walk a fine line between helping the police and protecting the movie.

She Talks to Angels
A Henry Malone Novel
James D.F. Hannah

Down & Out Books
May 2021
978-1-64396-173-6

2019 Shamus Award Nominee for Best Paperback Original!

Meadow Charles had plenty of secrets to hide—and someone left her dead in a land fill to keep those secrets hidden. The man who confessed to the crime now says he's innocent, and he needs Henry Malone to prove it.

Henry will have to explore one family's dark past—and confront someone willing to murder to keep those secrets buried!

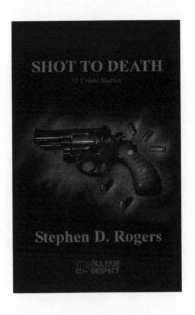

Shot to Death
31 Crime Stories
Stephen D. Rogers

All Due Respect, an imprint of
Down & Out Books
April 2021
978-1-64396-193-4

Thirty-one bullets that will leave you gasping for breath...

From hardboiled to noir to just plain human, these stories allow you to experience lives you escaped, and to do so with dignity, humor, and an eye toward tomorrow.

Misdeeds
A Criminal Collection of Crime Fiction
A.S. Coomer

Shotgun Honey, an imprint of
Down & Out Books
May 2021
978-1-64396-110-1

This is a book of *Misdeeds*. The stories between these covers will shock, appall, and enthrall.

There are killers in here. Thieves & vagabonds, needy sisters & disgruntled brothers, cops & kidnapers, not to mention a corruptor of children, all slide around the pages of *Misdeeds* like burning grease in an overheated pan.

These stories pop, sizzle, and burn. Consider yourself warned, fresh meat.

Made in the USA
Middletown, DE
01 October 2021